I HATE HOCKEY

François Barcelo

I HATE HOCKEY

Translated by Peter McCambridge

Baraka
Books
Montreal

Originally published under the title *J'haïs le hockey* by Les 400 coups

© Copyright for the original French edition François Barcelo and Les 400 coups.

 Canada Council   Conseil des Arts
for the Arts   du Canada

We acknowledge the support of the Canada Council for the Arts which last year invested $20.1 million in writing and publishing throughout Canada.

Book Design and Cover by Folio Infographie

Translation by Peter McCambridge

Library and Archives Canada Catalogue in Publishing

Barcelo, François, 1941-

[J'haïs le hockey. English]
I hate hockey / by François Barcelo; translated by Peter McCambridge.

Translation of: J'haïs le hockey.
ISBN 978-1-926824-13-0

1. McCambridge, Peter, 1979- II. Titre. III. Titre: J'haïs le hockey. English.
PS8553.A7615J4413 2011   C843'.54   C2011-906241-0

Legal Deposit, 4th quarter, 2011

Bibliothèque et Archives nationales du Québec
Library and Archives Canada

Published by Baraka Books of Montreal.
6977, rue Lacroix
Montréal, Québec H4E 2V4
Telephone: 514 808-8504
info@barakabooks.com
www.barakabooks.com

Printed and bound in Quebec

Trade Distribution & Returns
Canada
LitDistCo
1-800-591-6250; orders@litdistco.ca

United States
Independent Publishers Group
1-800-888-4741 (IPG1);
orders@ipgbook.com

1

I HATE hockey!

I've played just enough of it to know I'm the worst player ever. And I've watched just enough of it to know it's the worst sport ever.

I would of course have preferred for my son Jonathan to have had nothing to do with what I consider to be the most resounding expression of our national stupidity.

But Colombe, his mother, loves hockey and insisted on signing him up at the Saint-Zéphyrin Arena as soon as he turned six. She paid a fortune to get him equipped too. Resistance was futile—she was the one footing the bill.

Was that one of the reasons why we separated almost eight years later? I'm sure it was, even though Colombe insisted it had more to do with the fact that I had cheated on her with her accounting intern in the marital bed while she was with Jonathan and a few friends in a sports bar in the next town over, to spare me another Hockey Night in Canada on the family TV as it happened.

Six months ago I moved to Saint-Camille-de-Holstein, twelve kilometres from Saint-Zéphyrin. It's a village that you almost know. It lies behind the giant sheet-metal cow that stands on a hill you can see from the highway. I live in a miserable bachelor apartment above a closed-down gas station. It's the cheapest place in the neighbourhood, and every day it makes me hate hockey a little bit more.

So imagine my reaction when a man phones one Friday afternoon and begs me to coach my son's hockey team for an evening. It's Denis Beauchemin, president of the Saint-Zéphyrin Sports Association, which includes Saint-Camille since my new village doesn't have enough kids for its own school, let alone a hockey team. I protest and I don't even have to lie:

— But I HATE hockey. There's nothing I hate more.

— Listen, Mr. Vachon. We're really stuck here. The coach died suddenly last night.

I'm sure he expects me to ask how he died, but right away I imagine a coach with a big fat gut and a scrawny ass, a heavy beer drinker and no stranger to a bag of chips, succumbing to a heart attack while watching two hockey games on TV at once, thanks to the magic of picture-in-picture technology.

— The league requires us to have an adult behind the bench, he goes on. If there's no coach, we'll forfeit tonight's game.

— I'm sure there are other parents who could help. Ask my wife. She loves hockey. And she knows the game inside out.

He gives a deep throaty laugh.

— The government's come up with a new rule. Coaches of single-sex teams have to be the same sex as the players. They did it to have more women coaches. And it worked for synchronized swimming. But you can't have women in hockey because girls aren't allowed in boys' teams from bantam on.

I was six when my dad—who dreamed of seeing me play in the NHL—signed me up for a team. After just two games, my lack of talent was there for all to see and he pulled me from the team, mumbling something about the air in the arena not being good for my asthma.

Things were never the same between us after that. He never forgave me for forcing him to give up on his dream of having a famous hockey player for a son. Although my asthma did disappear almost right away, never to return.

I hated hockey for each of the thirty-three years that followed. Although I would still regularly be subjected to a few minutes of a game, which there's no getting around if you have the misfortune of living in Quebec. Especially for the fifteen years I lived with Colombe. She loved hockey and never missed a Habs game on TV, while I would make a beeline for the nearest bar. The game was always on there too, but at least I could sit with my back to the giant screen and ask them to turn the sound down.

But in all those years I've never found the game more unbearable than the evening I spent with my son in the so-called hockey Mecca that is the Bell Centre in Montreal.

My boss at the time—the well-to-do owner of a General Motors dealership—had given me two tickets. For four months in a row I'd sold more Saturns than anyone else in our area. And since he had Habs season's tickets, he felt he should give me a pair one night when the Minnesota Wild came to Montreal and when I reckon he really didn't feel like going on a one-hundred-and-thirty-kilometre roundtrip to go watch that.

I gave the tickets to Colombe, thinking that she'd go with our Jonathan, who had laced up his skates to play on his first team that year in our little town of Saint-Zéphyrin. But Colombe put her foot down. She couldn't possibly: this was a milestone in father-son relations. I gave in. And I regretted it as soon as we walked into the hallowed arena.

The game was of no interest whatsoever. Too few goals for my liking, as is nearly always the case with hockey. And the Wild won 2-1 to boot. But I hadn't expected the sport's merchandising to have reached such loud, in-your-face proportions.

Ads sped noisily around the rink on video screens right above our heads. The pre-recorded trumpet sounds were unbearably loud, as though the shouts from the crowd weren't enough to motivate the players. And music with no apparent connection to the game blared from loudspeakers. To top it all off, every time the action stopped for a TV commercial, we were pelted from all angles by deafening ads projected at the dazed crowd from every screen and amplifier in the building.

I felt bad about exposing my six-year-old son to such an abuse of marketing. Especially since I'd sworn to

Colombe that not a single beer would pass my lips. And Jonathan had promised his mom he'd tell on me if I cheated. But he was so wrapped up in the evening that he never mentioned the three beers I'd drunk for the price of a two-four from the store.

— And I suppose my son plays bantam.

— Nothing gets by you.

The president of the Saint-Zéphyrin Sports Association says it in such a way as to heap shame upon any father who has no idea to what level his son has progressed, if the concept of progress even comes into play in a sport like hockey. He goes on before I can find another reason to wriggle out of it.

— Half the players in Saint-Zéphyrin are Vietnamese. Their parents don't know the first thing about hockey. I managed to talk to a couple of dads who were actually born in Quebec, but Friday nights they work until six at the steel mill. And the bus needs to leave at four o'clock since the game is at eight in Morinville. They earn thirty-six dollars an hour; it's not like they're going to leave early. There's a policeman too, but he's on overtime this evening. For more than thirty-six dollars an hour, I bet. And all the other parents are single moms. You're my last hope. And Jonathan said you were between jobs.

Jonathan wasn't wrong. I lost my job when General Motors decided to get rid of Saturns. My boss, Gaston Germain, had promised I'd move on to Pontiacs if ever that happened because it had been coming for a while. Nurses and retired teachers drove Saturns and with my communications degree I was the only one who could talk to them, which was just as well since I was useless at selling trucks to farmers and the people who worked at the steel mill. Gaston Germain had promised me that when it was all over for Saturns I'd move on to Pontiacs. But GM got rid of Pontiacs too. Then they closed down a ton of dealers completely two days after I was sacked. I knocked on the door of every dealer between here and Montreal but nobody was hiring. So I told my son that I was between jobs. But that would only be entirely true if there were actually any prospects.

I protest again, hoping that my reluctance will at least get him to pay me for my evening's work:

— But I don't know anything about hockey. Line changes… the rules… anything!

— No problem! You have the best team in the league. The guys know the rules better than the refs. And your assistant can do the line changes. He has it all written down. All you have to do is stand behind the bench. If you can wear a tie, even better, but don't worry if you don't have one.

— Why doesn't the assistant coach fill in?

— He's aphasic. And he doesn't look like a coach.

I could point out that he's never seen me, but I have a better idea:

— Why don't you do it?

— I'm in a wheelchair and the school bus can't take me.

Talk about a great excuse. I mumble:

— I'm sorry. I didn't know.

— Listen, keep your arms folded for the whole game, if you like. Chew some gum and it'll look even better.

Just look pissed every time the ref makes a call. The guys will take care of the rest.

I keep on looking for another way out of it. If he's in a wheelchair, he can't come pick me up. I look at my watch: a quarter to four. I give it a try:

— I'd love to, but I moved to Saint-Camille a couple of months back. And I don't have a car. I don't see how I'll be able to get to Saint-Zéphyrin for four o'clock.

Barely have the words left my mouth when I realize they make no sense at all. He could tell me to take a taxI and they'll pay for it when I get there. Or they'll send someone to pick me up. But he goes one better:

— Look outside.

I walk over to the window: a yellow school bus is waiting outside by the pumps, which usually only attract drivers who come from too far away to know the garage has been closed for ages.

— Your school bus is waiting for you. Call me if you have any problems.

He gives me two numbers, his home number and his cell.

I throw on a jacket and tie as fast as I can. No need for a coat: it might be late October but we're still enjoying an Indian summer. I head down the stairs.

The bus door opens in front of me. I climb in. A man in his thirties is sitting behind the wheel. My assistant for the evening. I see right away why he'll never be a coach. He's wearing Coke bottle glasses and looks like he has a mild case of Down syndrome. He flashes me a smile so crooked it seems more like a wince. I say hello and force myself to look at him like he's perfectly normal. Then I take a look at my team: twenty or so boys fill the seats. There's Jonathan in the third row. He looks away and I guess he doesn't want the others to know I'm his dad. A fourteen-year-old boy could no doubt imagine few fates more terrible than having a dad who doesn't know the first thing about hockey for a coach.

The driver opens his mouth and says:

— Thi…

And then he goes quiet. My assistant is struggling to say something. It could be "the" or the start of any other word beginning with "thi," but I assume he wants to introduce me. I go on right away because my cousin Julie had a stroke last year and her husband told me that was the best thing to do with an aphasic.

— I'm your new coach, Antoine…

I can see Jonathan out of the corner of my eye. He's still pretending not to know me. I stop myself from saying my last name just in time. I even add (I hated it when Gaston Germain called me that, but with young people it's best to be as down-to-earth as possible):

— Call me Tony.

My team doesn't bat an eye. I have no reason at all to think they might be happy to see me. After all, if they were such a good team, their dead coach had surely played a part. He must have been their idol. Only a profiteering bastard would ever agree to replace him. It doesn't matter that I'm not being paid: in their eyes I'm nothing but a job stealer.

I walk down the bus to sit at the back, without so much as a look at Jonathan, who's still doing his best to ignore me, while the guy sitting next to him gives me a shy smile. He's Asian, like half the team.

A Vietnamese family came to live in Saint-Zéphyrin over thirty years ago when the farms and stores began to be left behind by the sons of the farmers and storekeepers gone to study to become doctors, teachers, and police officers in Montreal. The boat people opened a restaurant. The eldest boy bought a farm where to this day he still grows bok choy and any number of exotic vegetables I couldn't name if you paid me. Other Vietnamese—brothers, sisters, cousins, and distant relatives from the same village—followed them over, growing the same vegetables and opening Vietnamese, Cambodian, Chinese, and more recently Thai restaurants (because Thai food costs more, even when it's made by Vietnamese). Even more recently they launched a string of busy sushi restaurants, again making the most of Quebecers not being able to tell Southeast Asians and the Japanese apart. It's got to the point now that when you drive into town there is a big sign proudly proclaiming Saint-Zéphyrin "Quebec's Capital of Exotic Cooking."

They had more kids than we did and, thanks to Bill 101, their children and then their children's children are all perfectly integrated, which makes me hate hockey even more now that these foreigners—whether they were born here or not—have taken over our local teams. But don't tell anyone. My dislike of foreigners is just a venial sin compared to my hatred of hockey.

The school bus gets going, turning onto the road to Saint-Zéphyrin and then east along the highway.

When I was young, if there were twenty of us on a bus, we loved nothing more than a good singalong. And not just "Hail to the Bus Driver." We were also into more risqué songs like "Stop the Bus, I Need a Wee-Wee." But my team doesn't seem in the mood for singing or even talking for that matter. Maybe their dead coach didn't let them do either.

What am I meant to do for three hours on a bus? I don't know anything about my players. Time to find out more. As soon as the highway is straight enough for it to be safe to distract the driver, I get up to go talk to him:

— Beauchemin told me we have player records?

— H...

Here they are, pulled from his shirt pocket. I go back to my seat. There are five cards. Three forward lines (it's not written out but I guess as much because each line has three players: I don't know much about hockey but I know that much). And two lines of two defensemen. Each line has a number—1 to 3 for the forwards, 4 and 5 for the defensemen. The goalie doesn't have a line. It looks like he'll be playing the whole game.

To pass the time, I try to memorize the names. First line: K. Nguyen, Vachon, Latendresse-Provençal. Second line: Tremblay-Giroux, G. Nguyen, S. Nguyen. And so on. After half an hour, I can rattle off each line by heart without looking at it. The third line, for example: L'Heureux, R. Nguyen, Nguyen-Tremblay.

I'm ready.

I'm not ready at all. But at least I know the players' names and what line they're on. Tremblay-Giroux? Line 2, left wing since the names must be in order: left wing, centre, right wing.

You can't say I'm not taking my job seriously. My son plays centre on the first line, which you'll have noticed if I didn't forget to tell you my name's Antoine Vachon. And I bet the kid sitting next to him is on the same line. Left or right? Left, I'd say, because judging by his eyes he had more chance of being an Nguyen than a Latendresse-Provençal. But he's not super slanty eyed: Eurasian, or rather Quebecasian. The men of Saint-Zéphyrin have to marry Vietnamese if they want to get married. Our women would rather work for minimum wage in Montreal than become slaves to two hundred cows or marry steel workers who come home with grubby hands.

2

THREE HOURS and two hundred and thirty clicks later, here we are outside the Jean Dicaire Arena in Morinville. I suppose Jean Dicaire played in the NHL and that he came from this neck of the woods.

Sitting at the back, I wait until it's my turn to get off, amazed at the discipline of my players, who file out of the bus like passengers on an Airbus in Fort Lauderdale.

I follow them round to the back. Each takes his equipment bag, which has a Meteor logo on it. Is it the trademark of a canvas bag manufacturer or the team name: the Saint-Zéphyrin Meteors? I don't dare ask because it's unthinkable that the coach wouldn't know the name of his own team. I should have asked Beauchemin. Too late now. If the name has more than one syllable, my assistant will never be able to spit it out in anything like a reasonable amount of time. And there's no way I can let my players see I still don't know what their team's called—what my team's called. I'll find out soon enough when I see the jerseys.

Everybody has a bag, apart from me. All I have is a handful of papers in a jacket pocket. We follow the driver into the arena. He takes the hallway to his right, pushes open a door marked "Visitors," and we walk into our home for the evening.

Once again I admire my players' discipline. Their dead coach must have been a real law and order freak. Probably a retired cop or soldier. They get undressed in silence. Once they're in their boxers, they go into the showers and come back once they've put their jockstrap and pants on. I didn't think teens their age were so modest, but then I remember that Jonathan is like that on the weekends he stays with me. I haven't seen him naked for at least three or four years.

They're ready at last, helmets and gloves on, armed with skates and sticks. I'm the only one not ready. On the bus I thought long and hard about what I was going to say to them and I decided I wasn't going to say anything. If I open my mouth, no matter what I say, they're going to see that I know squat about hockey. They won't even look me in the eye anyways and don't seem to be expecting much from me. Maybe they used to have a quiet coach.

A siren—carefully chosen from among the most annoying imaginable—sounds… at length. My players get the message a few seconds before I do: it's time to head out onto the ice, not run away from a fire. They stand up and get in line. The driver/assistant opens the door. They go out. I follow them.

The other team has already started warming up on the rink. Their team name is emblazoned on the front of their jerseys: Loons. With a silhouette of the duck-like bird in the middle of a bronze-coloured circle that really does make the whole thing look not unlike a Canadian one dollar coin. But oh my God! The fans are blowing into a big trumpet type thing, and the sound recalls the bird's nerve-shattering cry.

Piss-poor name and logo if you ask me. But at least they have a name. My lot have only a letter on the front of their jerseys: Z. For Zenith, Zanies, Zephyrs? I have a hard time believing my team could be called the Saint-Zéphyrin Zephyrs. That's even worse than the Morinville Loons.

And our jersey is awful, if you ask me again. It's the very first time I've even seen a black and white team uniform. Like it had been designed before colour TV came along. With slightly crooked lines flying every which way. It looks like white lightning bolts on a black background. Without the Z, my money would have been on the Saint-Zéphyrin Lightning. Or how about the Zig-zaggers? The Zilches? The Zeroes? The Zonked Zombies? Nah, too funny. Hockey and humour have never gotten along well together.

Anyways, I'm probably the first coach of any sport in the history of mankind to start a game without knowing my team's name.

I realize there's worse to come when my players come back to sit on the bench after the warm-up. Because something equally catastrophic has just hit me: they don't have their names on the backs of their jerseys like the pros do. I have no way of telling who's who.

So here I am coaching a team whose name I don't know, with players I don't know (apart from my son, but when he's on the ice I still have a hard time telling him apart from the rest since his face is covered by his helmet and visor).

None of which would be too bad if I knew the first thing about hockey.

I know there are two teams, three thirty-minute periods, and that you score goals by putting the puck in the other team's net. But I know nothing about any of the rest of it. What are the two blue lines and the red line for? It's got something to do with offside, but I couldn't tell you what.

I have no choice: I'm going to play the role of the cool, calm, and collected coach who stands behind the bench with a smirk, fiddling with his chin. If I had gum, it would be even better. If I coach another game, I'll buy some. And I'll ask Beauchemin to pay me back.

My still anonymous assistant has taken his pile of notes back. He brandishes cards 1 and 4 and five players (including Jonathan) jump onto the ice.

If Jonathan plays centre on the first line, he must be one of the best. K. Nguyen, too, on the left wing, and Provençal-Latendresse on the right. At least learning the names of the players on each line hasn't been totally useless.

Except that if those three are my best forwards, we're going to get seriously hammered. They skate with no conviction and wait for the Loons to descend upon them and smack them into the boards. They don't even fight back. The second line is no better. Nor is the third. I have the world's worst players. Or else the other team is working hard. Yeah, that must be it: roared on by the partisan local crowd of fifty-odd parents, uncles, and complete strangers with nothing better to do, the Loons are going for blood, despite looking a bit shaky at times. Fortunately they couldn't get a shot on target if they tried, and while our goalie is making zero effort to stop the puck, it's not mattering much for the time being.

Just the once: a guy by the name of Dubois (did I mention the Loons have their players' names on their backs?) breaks away from my Jonathan and our K. Nguyen, then easily weaves his way between our two defensemen and releases a lacklustre shot that slides between the skates of our goalie, who hasn't even bothered keeping his stick on the ice, the one place where it might be of some use to him. This sets off a concert of Morinville vuvuzelas.

My team is playing so badly that I'm starting to see myself as a bit of a hockey connoisseur. After a few minutes of play, I've pinpointed all their weaknesses: they're nonchalant, lazy, slow, sadly lacking in stick-handling ability, useless at backchecking, and have no counter-attack. Even forechecking—which I would have real trouble explaining to you—seems to be as unfamiliar to them as it is to me.

The siren blares at last. At least the first half hour went by quickly. A quick glance at the scoreboard confirms it's 1-nothing for the Loons. Unfortunately, the scoreboard identifies us only as the Visitors, which leaves me none the wiser about my team's name.

We all traipse back into the "Visitors" locker room. And let me tell you what really gets my blood boiling (even though I couldn't care less about the result of this game of a sport I hate): my players aren't mad as hell. They show none of the signs of professionals who know they've played badly, especially when a camera lands on them. No faces like thunder, no sticks broken against the ice and boards. Not a single piece of gear thrown across the locker room in anger. My players don't seem happy or unhappy. It's worse: they're indifferent.

They sit in silence. I spend a few minutes wondering how I'm going to get them going. Because I have to admit—even though you might not believe me—I want them to win. Why? Hard to say. Because, whether they like it or not, they're my players now. Maybe for one night only, but it's still my team. As far as I remember, it's the very first time I've felt anything approaching team spirit. True, it's the first time I've been part of a team since I was six years old, and that's if you count the coach as part of the team.

But tonight a cripple put me in charge of his players. Sports matter to them. Hockey is maybe all that's stopping them from becoming delinquents and dropouts. I can hate the sport all I want, but I bet it's because of hockey that they make a bit of an effort at school if they don't want to be kicked off the team. Last spring, one Sunday afternoon when I asked him if he wanted to go for a bike ride, Jonathan said no: if he didn't get good grades, that would be the end of hockey for him. I feel responsible for them. Not just for Jonathan. For the twenty-odd boys I should be reminding that homework and studying is all very well, but sports are an even better school of life—even if I don't believe a word of it.

I can sense the siren coming soon to send them back out onto the ice. I get up and stand in front of the door to stop them leaving in case I don't have time to finish my speech:

— Listen, guys. I never got the chance to meet your coach…

I hesitate for a minute because I should say his name, or at least his first name, at the start of the next sentence. But I don't know either. Too bad.

— He was a good, demanding coach who knew how to get the best out of each of you. And I think you have to win the game tonight as a tribute to him. He deserves nothing less.

I'm in luck. The siren—which also isn't unlike the insufferable cry of a loon in search of a mate—breaks off my speech just as I wasn't sure what to say next.

The guys stand up. I get out of the way and they file past me solemnly. I'm sure they've gotten the message.

For a communications graduate, I must give the world's worst pep talks because they didn't understand a word of what I was expecting from them. I wanted them to play with at least a little intensity and grace. True, I might not necessarily have spelled it out for them. But I was sure they would understand. Playing without intensity or grace was going about the game the wrong way. Surely they understood that?

But they start to play like goons instead. Why? Don't ask me. That's not what I told them to do.

They send their opponents crashing into the boards, especially the smaller ones. It must all be perfectly legit, because the ref only dishes out four penalties. But that's enough for the other team to score two more goals.

With only a few minutes to go in the period (I've just found out there are twenty minutes in a period and I'm not going to argue), the Loons, understandably ticked at the way our players are getting on, worked up by a noisy crowd, and confident of winning the game no matter what, start hitting back. As hard as they like because the idiot of a ref doesn't react at all. My players are penalized for nothing at all, like tripping an opponent without meaning to, while the Loons go unpunished for blatant acts of violence, like slamming one of my smallest players into the boards.

One of them—Gervais, according to the name on his back—comes up behind our K. Nguyen, puts his stick between his legs, and sends him flying over the boards. Our Jonathan races over and smacks him one in the face. I would be proud of him if punching a shock-proof visor with a well-padded hockey glove was ever going to deter such a violent individual.

The two boys must have read my mind because they drop their sticks and gloves, fling their helmets to the ice, raise their fists, and get ready to box.

K. Nguyen's head pops back up over the boards and he gives a smile to show he's OK. But it's too late. All my players on the ice have already gone after the other team.

I've had enough. I might not be able to stop my team losing, but I'm not going to let them behave like a bunch of hooligans. I leap onto the ice. But I'm wearing my Saturn salesman shoes. The finest Italian shoes made in China, with the slipperiest of leather soles. I slide and fall on my ass, and that draws a laugh from the crowd.

Thankfully I'm close to the boards and I pull myself up and hang on for dear life. I call my players over:

— Get back here! Come back to the bench!

But no one can hear me over the laughs of the crowd. And they only laugh harder when I fall again. Just you try walking across ice with leather soles and we'll see who's laughing then.

I pick myself up, try my hardest not to fall again, push one of my Nguyens out of my way, and grab Jonathan by the ear. But he shakes his head loose and his fist makes solid contact with the nearest Loon.

I try to catch hold of him, but there's no point: he can skate faster than I can waddle.

Fortunately, everybody eventually grinds to a halt. Perhaps because I intervened. More likely because we're all hopelessly out of breath, exhausted like boxers in the tenth round. One by one, my players return to the bench, with me bringing up the rear because I've finally mastered the art of sliding my feet along the ice. I'm revving up to tear a strip off them, but I'm interrupted by a voice over the loudspeakers:

— Game misconduct to the coach of the visiting team for being the first to leave his bench to take part in a brawl.

Unless I'm very much mistaken, that's me, the coach of the visiting team. But I didn't do anything! I try to go over to the guy with the mike who just made the announcement to give him my side of the story. No chance: a real cop in uniform grabs hold of my arm and hauls me off in the opposite direction.

I just have time to glance across the ice at the other team's coach—a tieless fatso in a black jacket with an enormous loony on the front—who gives me the finger. OK, maybe I was asking for it a little.

— You can wait in the locker room, the police officer tells me, but if I see you near the rink again, I'll be bringing you down to the station.

The Loons have a 3–1 lead, according to the scoreboard over the hallway leading to the locker room. (We had gotten one goal back by accident when our goalie cleared the puck straight into the Loons' net.)

It's a complete and utter embarrassment. I would go home, if I could. But I have no way of getting home. There's no chance of an adult male finding a sympathetic driver to pull over at the side of the highway in the dark. Our bus is the only way home. I find a copy of the local paper in the locker room and discover the Loons have yet to win a single game. Fair enough, it's only October, but they've still lost five. Saint-Zéphyrin is ranked first out of eight teams, with five wins and no losses before tonight.

My team of losers for the evening joins me in the locker room. They sit down. A few of them give me a smirk. They're clearly going to have me take the blame for the loss. They've found an original way to pay tribute to their dead coach: lose pathetically with the new one. I find it unbelievably stupid, but it's perfectly understandable.

After a long period of reflection, I decide to tell them a few home truths. I stand up. No need to call for quiet: no one's said a word.

— I have a confession to make: I HATE hockey.

That's how I said it: I HATE hockey. Because when you hate hockey like I hate hockey, you can say "I HATE hockey" all you like.

— If I'm here with you tonight, it's because they couldn't find anybody else. I'm unlucky enough to have fathered one of you and President Beauchemin had my phone number. I won't say which of you is mortified at being my son.

The glances at the few Quebec-born players confirm that Jonathan isn't suspected of being my kid any more than the others. The little devil even glances around himself to divert suspicion. I go on:

— He called me, said you were the best team in the league, that you couldn't lose. He's in for a surprise when he finds out I managed it. But I can't complain because it means I won't ever have to coach you again, if you can call this coaching.

The loon's lament makes itself heard one more time.

— Go ahead. I'll wait for you here. Because I have to.

The players get up and leave sheepishly. Perhaps a little ashamed as well. No. I bet they're trying their best not to smirk. They've always won under a demanding coach, maybe a tyrant, and now they have the luxury of losing a game and pointing the finger at their new coach, who can't stand hockey. I should just have kept my big mouth shut.

I stay in my seat in the locker room, under the murky fluorescent lights. I try to think about my life, which isn't exactly a barrel of laughs. The ups and downs of my coaching career should be the least of my problems.

I'm thirty-nine, going through a divorce, father of a fourteen-year-old son I can't seem to talk to. I have a degree in communications, but that didn't get me far when I arrived on the scene after tens of thousands of other people with communications degrees had already snapped up all the interesting jobs. I went back to the town where I grew up. I sold cars for General Motors, convinced that the world's biggest company would never have to worry about going bankrupt. I married the first girl who said yes. And here I am, an out-of-work divorcee who can't find another job. I don't have a car anymore and I live in a lousy apartment no one else would ever take. I don't even have a girlfriend and I'll never find one because everyone knows that any girl after a stable relationship avoids unemployed losers like me like the plague. Anyway, I don't even want a girlfriend. No more than I want to have friends. They'd only pity me, and the more pitiful you are, the less you feel like being pitied. To top it all off, I'm two months behind with my rent. I'd happily contemplate suicide, if I wasn't sure I'd make a real mess of that too.

Maybe I'll become homeless. Can you be happy without a roof over your head? I've seen a few happy ones, waiting for lunch outside the soup kitchens in Montreal. You know, I don't think it would be too bad. I could spend my days with my arm out in front of the Metro station, happy enough with one or two free meals, scraping together just enough to buy myself a few bottles of beer with the money passers-by give me for coffee, trying to sleep at night among the schizophrenics and the paranoid and becoming that too, if you can be both at once. Cavemen, most people in the Middle Ages and the industrial revolution, and nearly everyone living today in Haiti, Congo, and Zimbabwe—they were all dealt a worse hand than that.

I've been reduced to consoling myself by drawing comparisons when the locker room door opens. My ex-assistant strides in, a broad grin across his face. He's followed by the members of my ex-team, overjoyed and boisterous. I barely recognize them.

— Sssiii...

— 6–3, a dozen players shout at once.

— Kim got a hat trick, someone says.

I'm nearly as proud of myself as I am of Kim: I know that means he scored three goals. Or maybe four.

Anyway, I don't understand much else for a while. The team chatters away as the players take off their uniforms and dress up as teenagers again. Unless I'm completely wrong, my team rallied in the third period. Why? Was it something I said? But what did I say? Nothing likely to make winners out of losers. Maybe they realized just in time they really couldn't lose, no matter who was coaching them.

3

WE GET BACK on the bus. The atmosphere is relaxed. The players still aren't singing. They talk at least, just not to me.

It's almost ten o'clock. I suppose we're going to have to drive every player back and it'll be up to me to look after them until every last one has returned to the family home. I won't be in bed until two or three o'clock. Too late for a drink at the bar, where I've already overextended my credit in unpaid drinks.

The bus starts. Before hitting the highway, we pass by a Tim Hortons. If I had more than ten dollars in my pocket I would invite my team to celebrate our win (yes, our win, since there's no proof it would have happened if I hadn't woken them up with my game misconduct). But the driver hasn't spotted the sign for Montreal to the right. Instead we continue along the overpass that crosses over the highway. I get up to go tell him he's missed the turn, but just as I get close, he turns left before I've had a chance to open my mouth and stops a few metres further on in front of the MoreInnTown Motel.

— We...

— We're going to sleep here?

He nods, delighted that he only needs to say a half or even a quarter of a word and I understand, even if just this once he managed a whole one. He takes out a set of keys from a small leather pouch, each attached to an oval keychain with a number on it. He gives me No. 19 and points to the end of the motel, the furthest away from the reception. I get it. He's taken care of booking twenty rooms for the team and all I have to do is walk over to mine. Beauchemin could have given me a bit of a heads-up. I would have brought a toothbrush and pyjamas. But I sleep in my boxers at home and that'll do just fine. And it won't be the first time I go to bed without brushing my teeth.

Handing out twenty keys is probably going to take forever and I'm exhausted without really knowing why. I shout, "Night, guys!" and head off to Room 19.

There are two Queen beds with ill-matched eiderdowns. It could do with a lick of paint, the carpet could have a few less stains, and the landscape prints on the walls could be less tasteless, but all in all it'll be fine for a night.

I take off my jacket and tie. I turn on the TV but the news has already started and I don't like watching when I've missed all the important stuff at the beginning. I turn off the TV. I give the bed closest to the bathroom a squeeze. The mattress seems OK.

But I'm starving. I haven't eaten since lunchtime. The kids probably have a bite to eat in their bags: chocolate bars, cookies, energy drinks, and the like. I've got nothing. I'll just run over to Tim Hortons on the other side of the highway. No one should see me in the dark.

I'm just about to put my jacket back on when there's a knock at the door. I open it.

It's K. Nguyen. What does he want? He holds up a key with the same number as mine to show me we're going to be sharing the room for the night. Too bad. For him especially—there's no way he'll be able to out-snore me.

He throws his bag in the corner, takes out a small travel bag, and heads toward the bathroom.

There's another knock on the door. Are you kidding me? There's going to be four of us—in two beds. The driver could have told me, even if he would have needed half an hour.

Speak of the devil. He's holding out a square box that can only contain pizza, especially since it has a Pizzeria Morino logo on it.

— Piii...

— Pizza, I get it.

He gives me a broad smile, then closes the door.

I set the pizza down on the small table between the two chairs. K. Nguyen comes over to join me. I suppose he didn't brush his teeth because he knew that pizza was a post-game ritual. Or at least after every win. Or maybe just when we play on the road and end up starving in a motel.

The pizza isn't very big—ten or twelve inches, I guess— but it should be enough for two. I put half each on the two cardboard plates. And we eat in silence. What can you say to a player who's just scored three goals when you didn't see a single one of them? K. Nguyen is shy and doesn't have anything to say either.

To make conversation, I ask him:

— Is it always you that rooms with the coach?

— No. Sometimes it's Jonathan.

Did Jonathan tell my assistant he didn't want to share my room? Or did it just turn out like that? Jonathan rooms with the coach every other time and it was his turn last time?

K. Nguyen throws the empty plates, plastic cutlery, and cardboard box into the wastepaper basket and goes back to brush his teeth. I get undressed and slide between the sheets while his back is turned. I keep my boxers on. You're not going to catch me walking about naked in front of a minor. Social services wouldn't be pleased.

He comes back wearing huge pyjamas that look like they belong to his dad.

He gets into the other bed and I turn off the bedside lamp.

I can't fall asleep first. I don't want Jonathan's teammates to find out his dad snores like a freight train the day when I don't know what will force him to admit we're related. Because now that I think about it, I'll maybe try my hand at coaching the team again. The other coach is still dead, and it can't be easy replacing a coach or else I wouldn't be here. Plus, coaching a hockey team would be fun, something to get the old adrenaline going in my spare time, which, let's face it, isn't going to be in short supply any time soon. It would help me meet people, especially when we play in Saint-Zéphyrin.

Single mothers, for instance, since I'm too old to be running around after young things (Colombe's accounting intern was in her thirties). Abandoned mothers aren't as hard on the unemployed as the young, free, and single. Welfare bums would be even more understanding, but I'm planning on aiming a little higher than that. Coaching a winning team—and why wouldn't it keep on winning under me when it can win very well without me?—will make me look like a fighter. And not just to single moms: dads who don't have time to watch their offspring in action away from Saint-Zéphyrin will all think so too. I'll maybe get offered a job managing a sports store, or a sushi counter, or even a team that can afford to pay its coach.

You don't need to be a great expert to coach a team—I wasn't even there for the triumphant third period. I could get promoted. First by following Jonathan. Next year he'll be playing midget, I think, unless he'll stay bantam for another year. After that I don't know. Junior maybe, unless there's something between midget and junior. And if he ever makes it to the NHL, I could try and be the team's trainer. Or equipment manager. And wind up assistant coach. After that, the sky's the limit, as they say.

I'm dreaming in colour while I'm still wide awake, and I get the feeling that my dreams are going to get even better once I fall asleep. Even the best-looking ladies are interested in an NHL coach. Weathergirls, models, actresses, anybody at all with a chest to die for.

That's all great, but I'm really going to need some shut-eye if I'm going to have time to dream all I like.

My dreams—yours too, I suppose—have been in 3D since well before 3D movies came out. Huge breasts in 3D are almost better than the real thing.

But I can't sleep. What time is it? The battery in my Timex is too weak to light up the watch face. There's an alarm clock on the only bedside table between the two beds. But I still can't see the time because it's facing the wrong way. I get up to move it back. And I see K. Nguyen's face faintly lit up by the greenish hue of the display. Already seventeen minutes past midnight. My roommate opens his eyes when I turn the alarm clock round to face my bed. He says, in the voice of a teen that still hasn't broken, but is surely about to any minute:

— I only do blow jobs.

I'm stunned. Put yourself in my place. I stay standing for a second or two, trying to make out K. Nguyen's face, which is no longer lit up by the alarm clock. Perhaps you're thinking I'm trying to make up my mind. It could be that because, ashamed as I am to admit it, I like nothing more than a blow job from time to time. Colombe wasn't a big fan. So I've been longing for one for a while now. I also have to admit that in the six months we've been separated I've yet to entice a girl back to my bed. And even though you can get a blow job in lots of other places outside of a bed (in a car, for example, if I still had one) it still hasn't happened.

It must be said I haven't been looking very hard. I spent the first few months feeling sorry for myself. I've just decided it's time to start putting my life back together. But the hunting season hasn't officially reopened yet. I'm happy enough to go to Chez Camille, a bar where there aren't too many good-looking women, apart from the bartender who's going out with Sylvain Ménard, my landlord. And if I get on the wrong side of him, I'm going to get kicked out of the bar and my apartment at the same time.

So I wouldn't say no to a blow job and I think it over for a few seconds. No longer than ten, anyway. I'm not sure about a boy. In theory, it's the same thing: a guy's mouth or a girl's mouth is still a mouth—it's the same inside and should feel the same. I bet if you closed your eyes you couldn't tell the difference. But I don't want to, even if K. Nguyen does look a bit effeminate.

Especially not a blow job from a minor.

Especially since I'm his coach, at least until we get back to Saint-Zéphyrin. I'm in a position of authority here. I doubt a judge would find me being thrown out of the game would change very much if ever I did end up in court. And even if K. Nguyen says I just let him get on with it (after all, he was the one that brought it up) I'm still looking at a couple of years behind bars, where pedophiles get fucked every night, to help them get over their perversion. And even if K. Nguyen says nothing now, that's not going to stop him pressing charges in ten or twenty years' time when I've rebuilt my life with a new job and a new family and it's going to be even more trouble then. That kind of thing has happened before, and it's on the rise.

I go back to bed without saying a word. I pretend to be asleep, hoping my silence will be enough to contain my roommate's appetite. And it works: K. Nguyen doesn't try again. Great. Or too bad.

I still can't sleep. First, because there's something weird about "I only do blow jobs." Does that mean he doesn't want to be buggered? Or to sodomize his partner for the night? Not surprising. AIDS has seen oral sex rise in the popularity stakes and sodomy fall. Plus, I imagine a thirteen- or fourteen-year-old's ass must be a bit on the small side for a coach turning forty.

But that's not really what's bugging me. I can't get something else out of my head. If K. Nguyen said that, it must be because my lately departed predecessor indulged in that kind of post-game treat. And he must have done it to him, otherwise K. Nguyen would never have told me to keep it to blow jobs. My predecessor must have assaulted him in exchange for ice time. And ice time is what every young hockey player needs, you don't need to be an expert to know that. The more time you spend on the ice, the more goals you score. It's simple math. I bet Wayne Gretzky had all the ice time he wanted when he played bantam. What did he do to earn it? I don't know if you remember photos of him when he was younger, but he looked a bit effeminate too.

And suddenly—horror of horrors!—I remember K. Nguyen telling me Jonathan sometimes roomed with the coach too. There's only one possible conclusion: my son has been sexually assaulted!

Blow jobs or buggery? Probably both. No wonder he's playing centre for the best left-winger on the team. Because you need more than just ice time to become a great hockey player: you need great line-mates too. You

40

can be as talented as you want: if your wingers or centre are bad, you're not going to go very far. Even Gretzky must always have played with the team's best players. For players, it's worth being molested if that means getting to play pro, or going on to be a top scorer, if they're already NHLers.

And the whole thing is Colombe's fault. Not for Gretzky, of course, just Jonathan. She was the one who signed him up for hockey before he was even seven. Despite what I thought. I'd signed him up for swimming lessons. And no one's ever heard of swimming instructors not being able to keep their hands off young swimmers. They're happy enough getting to watch little boys and girls run about in ultra-tight swimsuits. They're voyeurs, but at least they don't feel the kids up.

Now before you say it, I know Colombe didn't do it on purpose. She never thought for a minute that her son's hockey coach would be going around demanding blow jobs from him. Or worse. But the fact remains that everything that has happened to our son is her fault.

What am I going to do now? Should I talk to Jonathan? I'm not sure that I should. He must be feeling unbelievably ashamed. Too ashamed to talk to his parents. And I must be right because he hasn't. Not even to his mom, otherwise Colombe would have told me. It's the type of thing you talk to your ex about if he's the father of your children. Nothing beats it for making him feel guilty about running out on you, even if it was you that kicked him out. I'll have a word with Colombe tomorrow—no today, it's after midnight. I'll try and convince her to take him out of hockey and pay for a psychiatrist. Psychiatrists must cost a hell of a lot more than hockey. But you must be able to get over a trauma like that, if you catch it in time. Will she believe me? She'll pretend not to because hockey was her idea.

At least the coach is dead. But I'll have to stay on as coach if Jonathan keeps on playing. If they replace me, who says they're not going to choose some other pedophile. Everyone knows that men who like young boys go for jobs where they can be near them: scout leaders, priests, hockey coaches.

I've half a mind to call this dumbass Beauchemin and beg him to let me stay before he hears about my on-ice antics. We won but, oh, by the way, I got a game misconduct. I'll have to explain everything to him asap. But have I got his number? I seem to remember writing it down on a scrap of paper and putting it in my wallet.

I go to the bathroom, picking my pants off the floor on the way. I turn the light on and close the door behind me so I don't wake K. Nguyen. My wallet is in my back pocket. Yes, I have his number. His numbers: he gave me his cell number too.

Which should I call? The landline: at this time of night he's sure to be in bed. But he said to call any time at all if I had a problem. And right now I have problems. Worse: a big problem. I won't bring it up, just ask him to keep me on as coach. Is it OK to call the president of a sports association after midnight about something like that? Of course not. I leave Beauchemin's numbers beside the phone and go back to bed.

It's Saturday and I'd rather talk to him at a reasonable hour. Nine o'clock in the morning is perfectly reasonable. Although we'll probably be back on the bus then. I'll call him as soon as I get home. In the meantime, I'll try and get some sleep.

But I still can't sleep because now I've started to wonder about something else: how did the other coach die? "Suddenly." That's all Beauchemin said. But there are a million ways to die suddenly. In a car accident or a plane wreck. Of a heart attack or a stroke. You can also commit suicide or get knocked off—two ways to end it all that would fit perfectly with the life of a pedophile.

I would call right away to clear the whole thing up but K. Nguyen is in the bed next to me and I might wake him up. I get up with the phone all the same in case the cable is long enough for me to be able to call him from the bathroom with the door closed. It isn't.

You're going to say I'm quick off the mark, but here I am standing in the middle of the night in the phone booth opposite the motel. I've got no change and my credit cards are maxxed out. But Beauchemin must be able to afford a collect call.

Yes! He says "Yes," resigned or indifferent, to the mechanical voice that asks if he will accept a collect call from Antoine Vachon.

— What the hell do you want? he barks. I know you won. 6–3. Not 11–1 like last week, but not too bad for an away game.

— Who told you? I ask, as politely as I can manage.

— It was on the radio in Taschereau. They said you got kicked out of the game too. Good idea, that. It'll give you more authority over the young bucks. They like coaches with balls.

Good news: sounds like I'm still coach without even having to ask.

— So whaddya want? he says. You know what time it is?

— I just have a question.

I have a good dozen, but I make do with this one:

— How did the other coach die?

There is a moment's hesitation, then a sigh, then he says:

— Don Moisan? He was murdered. Beaten to death with a baseball bat, if you really want to know.

— Ah OK!, I say, as though relieved to know he didn't die of a heart attack. Who did it?

— The police would like to know too.

— Any leads?

— Have to ask them.

I shut up, trying hard to think of another sensible question. And also because I'm scared Beauchemin is starting to think I bumped off my predecessor to get his job.

— Can I go back to bed now? my president asks from the other end of the line.

— Yes.

I go back to bed as well.

As I walk back to the motel, I try to imagine Jonathan hitting a man over the head with a baseball bat. I can't do it, because I don't know where the murder took place. And it's hard to imagine something when you don't have a clue what the crime scene looked like. In the coach's bed? Out on the street? In a motel? On his lawn as he

44

was cutting the grass for the last time this year and with the noise of the lawnmower he didn't hear Jonathan sneaking up on him?

No, I'm pretty sure yesterday afternoon Beauchemin told me he had died the night before. You don't mow your lawn in the middle of the night in late October.

I don't even know where this Don Moisan character lived. In a bungalow? In a house in the country? In an apartment? In Saint-Zéphyrin or one of the neighbouring villages? There's nothing saying an unpaid coach has to live in the same town as his team. Was he even unpaid? Am I? Beauchemin hasn't mentioned it. I almost feel like calling him back to ask. But there's no point. He'll never accept a collect call a second time.

At any rate, these are all mere details when you think about what I'm up against now. My son might have murdered someone. He had a motive: his coach was forcing oral sex on him, and—who knows?—all kinds of other disgusting stuff. Jonathan had the murder weapon because he plays baseball every summer. Since he gave up swimming, I'm even the one that pays for it because it costs a lot less than hockey, which is more in line with Colombe's budget, and I hate baseball a hundred times less than I hate hockey. It has to be said that my dad never forced me to play baseball. And the Expos had already left Montreal before Jonathan was old enough for me to take him to see them.

So my son is maybe—probably—a murderer. Although circumstances don't get much more mitigating than that. Especially if he made him do more than oral, like K. Nguyen. Fortunately he's a minor and that'll earn him at

45

most a few years in one of those youth centres they used to call reform schools. I don't know why they changed the name. If you ask me, if I was Jonathan's age the thought of getting locked up in a youth centre wouldn't scare me half as much. Not enough to put me off killing someone who was molesting me anyway.

But there's enough there to ruin a life. Getting raped by your coach is so shameful that the only hockey players to ever admit it only said something ten or twenty years later, when their careers were well over. And you can say what you like, but a past as a teenage murderer isn't going to impress prospective employers or girlfriends.

I'm not the perfect father. You might already have noticed, whether you're a better parent than me or not. But that doesn't stop me making up my mind to do the impossible so that Jonathan isn't ever suspected let alone arrested. How? First, I'll have a word with him. He'll deny everything, but I know him and I'll be able to see if he's telling the truth or not.

I could go to his room right now. But I don't know which one he's in. And I'm not going to risk waking everyone up. Nobody knows I'm his dad and questions will be asked if I start knocking on all the doors, calling out his name.

I'll wait until everybody's up and take him to one side for a minute or two. Maybe at breakfast. He doesn't want anybody to know I'm his dad, but a coach has the right to a private meeting with one of his players. It never bothered my predecessor, by the looks of things.

For the time being, I'll try to get a few hours' sleep to clear my head. But as I stand outside the door to

Room 19, I can look in my pockets all I like, I can't find my key. I must have left it on the bedside table inside.

I turn the handle, but I'm out of luck: the door locked behind me when I went out earlier. Like it or not, I'm going to have to wake K. Nguyen. I knock gently, then put my ear to the door. Not a sound. I try again, a little louder this time. Still nothing. Should I yell? I'm only going to wake someone up or alert an insomniac in one of the neighbouring rooms. If it's not one of my players, he's going to wonder what the wino outside's playing at, shouting in the middle of the night. And if it is one of my players, it's not going to be much better.

My third attempt, hitting barely any harder than the time before but eight times instead of three, gets results. I hear someone moving around. A few seconds later, I see K. Nguyen's slightly slanty eyes peering at me through the half-open door.

I whisper:

— I forgot my key.

He lets me in, asks no questions, and I give no answers. He closes the door and we're back in the dark again. We go back to bed, each on our own side.

Should I ask him or not? When it comes down to it, he's as likely to have killed Don Moisan as my Jonathan. He was molested too, you know. But he doesn't look like he'd ever do anything like that.

No doubt you're having trouble imagining that a father could ever think his fourteen-year-old son had the look of a murderer about him. That's because you haven't been in my head for the past hour as I play the film I've imagined for myself over and over again (even

47

if I've no idea where the murder takes place): Jonathan, baseball bat in hand, hits a guy over the head who raises his hands to protect himself, then drops his guard as blood trickles down his head and a grin lights up my son's face.

If you have kids yourself, just try to imagine one of them—doesn't matter which one, but preferably the one that looks most like a murderer—killing a stranger or even your best friend. I bet it won't take you more than a few minutes. Even if she's a delicate little flower. Imagine anything at all for long enough and it becomes plausible. But it doesn't work with K. Nguyen. He has very dainty features for a hockey player. He's thin, a bit effeminate like all Asians his age, maybe a bit more than them if they only half look like girls. I can try to picture him murdering someone all I want: I can't do it. Now, you'll say I wouldn't have been able to imagine him playing hockey either if I hadn't already seen him in uniform, but that's not the same thing at all.

If you know anything about the odds of probability, I'd say there are nine chances out of ten that Jonathan did it and just the one for K. Nguyen. I hear him moving in the bed beside me. He's no doubt my son's best buddy. He must know what's being going on. Maybe he was even there, maybe he tried to stop him, but Jonathan was so worked up he couldn't do anything.

I might as well ask him, just to be sure:

— I've a question for you. I'd like you to be straight with me. Was it Jonathan?

He hesitates a few seconds before admitting:

— Yes.

He says it with a sob, then bursts into tears. What should I do now? Hop into bed with him and give him a hug? No thanks. That could be held against me if ever he's asked if Don Moisan was the only one to hold him in his arms. — No, Tony Vachon did it too, in the middle of the night, in a motel in Morinville.

I'm no good at dealing with other people's feelings anyways. I can't remember holding Jonathan against me since he was, I don't know, seven or eight. Or six. In my family, men were men. No time to be lovey-dovey, no tears, no signs of affection (ambiguous and pointless). No point saying I love you when it's obvious you do. And if you don't love each other, then why lie?

K. Nguyen soon stops crying anyway. And you won't see me complaining.

4

I open my eyes. I think I was asleep. It's still dark. The radio alarm clock shows 05:30. I can't believe I spent all those hours racking my brains over Jonathan's fate.

Hey, there's a funny light behind the curtains. A reddish light that's coming and going like it was flashing. I have a bad feeling about this.

I get up without making a sound and lift part of the curtain. It's just as I feared: the flashing light belongs to the cops. There are three SQ police cars parked in front of the reception. One of them has its lights flashing. The two others don't, but that's even more worrying, if you ask me.

There are times in a father's life when he has to stand up and act like a father. You can call it facing up to his responsibilities, if you prefer to sound all serious. No doubt you think it's a father's responsibility, when his son is wanted for murder in a civilized country, to hand him over to the cops in a heartbeat. Accidents happen so easily, after all. An arrest or a police chase can go wrong with our trigger-happy young guns these days, with nearly as many women as men among their ranks.

I must admit that if I did hand Jonathan over to the cops, nothing too bad could happen to him. He would appear before a youth court, his lawyer would plead mitigating circumstances (and you can hardly think of better mitigating circumstances than a hockey coach sexually assaulting a young boy who's just turned fourteen, if it didn't start even earlier). But just suppose—worst-case scenario—he gets two or three years in a youth centre. It wouldn't be too bad. He'd be surrounded by highly trained staff and able to study just as well as if he had kept on living with his mom and gone to Taschereau High, where sex, drugs, bone-idleness, and I don't know what else lie in store for him.

But what would he think of me? Especially since I handed him over to cops whose interrogation methods surely don't change depending on their victim's age. Jonathan has all the innocence of youth and might end up confessing to something worse. They might get him to say he made the first move and tried to seduce that bastard Moisan. And even if it was true, there's no way I could let him do that. Mitigating circumstances don't last very long when they come up against skilled investigators and overzealous prosecutors who are chomping at the bit to be judges.

There's no way I can hand him over. No way I can let him sleep on until the cops who have come to arrest him have searched every room either. How do they know it was him? All the players, not counting my assistant, must have known he was rooming with the coach. Or maybe that little asshole K. Nguyen has been shooting his mouth off. If he's prepared to accuse Jonathan to my face (when he thinks I'm a complete stranger, not the murderer's father) he's probably been telling his teammates the same.

I need to get my son out of here and find him a lawyer before the cops get their hands on him. The problem is it's Saturday and lawyers don't work weekends. That's why they went into law and not medicine, after all. Colombe might know somebody. She's an accountant, she's been an expert witness in fraud trials. Surely she can recommend me a lawyer who's less incompetent than the rest.

I get dressed again, thinking it all over, and ask K. Nguyen, who I can see is looking at me in the dark:

— You know what room he's in?

— Right beside us.

This time I remember to put the key in my pocket on the way out. I knock on Room 18. A boy opens the door with a yawn. It's not Jonathan. Maybe K. Nguyen was wrong.

— Is Jonathan there?

— Yes, says my son's voice.

I push the door open. By the light of the street lamp outside, I can see him lying on the bed. There's no one in the other bed, which has been slept in. I'm reassured: he's not gay. Or he's not sleeping with his roommate at any rate. At least not this one. Which isn't to say he's not too close to K. Nguyen. That would be Don Moisan's fault too. And more or less Colombe's and hockey's fault as well. I tell him:

— Quick, get dressed. The police are outside.

The other guy behind me must look surprised because Jonathan feels obliged to tell him:

— He's my dad.

That makes me happy. He can't be completely ashamed of me: he's just told his teammate I'm his dad. Especially after my game misconduct. But no doubt he can't think of any other way to explain why some guy has come to pick him up in the middle of the night.

Jonathan doesn't protest and starts to get dressed.

I say to the other boy:

— If anyone asks you where we went, you tell them someone came to pick us up in a car around midnight. In a green car, OK?

Colombe has a green Honda. Is that going to get her into hot water? Probably. I don't say it just because it's fun to, but because desperate times call for desperate measures. If the cops have to spend a few hours trying to get Colombe to confess to dropping us off somewhere, it will buy us some time. And if they think we've been gone for six hours, they'll look much further than we'll be if we leave at six in the morning.

I've never seen Jonathan get dressed so fast. When he stays with me, it takes him at least half an hour to get ready for school. But he's ready in under a minute. If you want your kid to get dressed in a hurry, just tell him the police are after him.

— Tell Kim to take my gear, my son tells his friend.

I'll never understand the kids of today. I tell Jonathan the cops are on his tail and he's worried about his hockey gear. Unless maybe the baseball bat used in the murder is in there?

If I had time to lose, I'd try and hide it somewhere it wasn't likely to be found. But I can't see any good hiding places. May as well leave it where it is, if it is there.

I take a peek out the half-open door. The cops are still standing there beside the three cars. They're too far away for me to make out what they're saying. Are they waiting for backup? There are four of them, if my math is right, and that seems more than enough to arrest a kid of fourteen if you ask me, even if he is protected by his dad. There's not a minute to lose.

— Follow me.

I pop out the door and take a left, away from the reception. Jonathan is behind me. My room is the last one in the row. I go round the back. Behind the motel, there's bush. Maybe a big forest even. Better walk through the bush than along the road. I'm sure cops would rather chase after murderers in their cars rather than on foot. Where are we going anyway? The only thing I know for sure is that I have to buy some time and a forest big enough to get lost in seems the perfect place.

It's almost dawn. But it's still pitch dark in under the trees, even though they've lost almost all their leaves. I start to run, trip, Jonathan helps me back up like I was an old man. I don't say thanks. Just "Sssh!" like he was the one making noise.

I start running again, and go over again. Again it's the fault of my damned car salesman's shoes, the ones I thought would really look the part on a hockey coach. The ones that aren't any better suited to a muddy forest trail than a freshly Zambonied rink. I bet the other coach—whose feet I never saw—wore Nikes to lead his team. I should've done the same.

I get back up and make a sign to Jonathan to slow down. We walk for I don't know how long through the bush until we reach a clearing. As we get closer, I see it's a train track that runs along an embankment, at least a metre higher than the trail. We get even closer and I see there's a mesh-wire fence standing in our way.

A few more steps and we come to a halt in front of the fence. No doubt it's there to stop pedestrians from crossing the train tracks to get to the McDonald's on the other side. I can see its golden arches just a few hundred metres away. I suppose a couple of teenagers got knocked down trying to cross. The fence must be brand new because no one's had time to put a hole in it big enough for us to pass through.

My watch says it's ten to seven. It's bright, even though we can't see the sun yet.

What are we going to do? I don't have to think long. Story book images of father and son hopping on the back of a freight train and crossing the country to get away from the cops spring to mind. If they haven't made a movie about that yet, they should have. Yeah, I'm up for that. It's not as if I'm going to ruin my non-existent career. And if ever they catch up with us, I'm pretty sure I'm looking at no more than a suspended sentence for helping my son go on the lam, given the circumstances. I'll ask the judge, "What would you have done if it had been your son?" He won't answer because judges don't like answering defendants' questions, but he'll be shaken.

— Can you jump over the fence?

In reply, he leaps over it like a squirrel up a tree, without me even having to give him a boost.

I just have to do the same. I hang on to the fence with both hands and lift myself up a bit. But my feet are no help. Jonathan was wearing soft running shoes, with a tip that fit in the holes of the fence and a tread that held on to the wire. I'm wearing my car salesman's shoes, with a more or less square tip that's too broad to fit into the fence. Plus I weigh over a hundred kilos, not forty-five. After a couple of failed attempts, with me not getting more than a metre off the ground, I make up my mind:

— We'll walk along the fence on either side. There's bound to be a hole somewhere. Or a crossing gate.

I head left. The overpass for Morinville is on that side. Who knows, in the other direction there might not be an opening in the fence for ten or twenty kilometres.

We walk two or three metres apart, separated by the wire fence. It doesn't help the conversation any, even if we can both hear each other. Try it if ever you get the chance. Hard to talk about paternal love—or any other kind for that matter—when you're separated like that. Psychological barriers are often the hardest to get over, as any psychiatrist will tell you.

— So what did you do, Dad? asks Jonathan after a hundred steps or so in silence.

— What do you mean?

— Well they didn't send the cops because of the brawl. Don Moisan did much worse and there was never a problem.

I can't believe it. For a second I think Jonathan is maybe trying it out, trying to get me to think the cops are after me, not him. But his voice sounds so sincere—especially with something resembling compassion for his dad, impossible to fake—that I believe him. The cops aren't here because of him. He doesn't seem to think so anyway. If he'd killed someone, he'd know the cops were after him, not me. So he can't have killed anyone. Better check to be on the safe side.

— You didn't kill Moisan then?

Jonathan bursts out laughing.

— No! What made you think that?

— Your left winger told me.

— Kim told you that?

— Yup.

K. Nguyen is called Kim, nothing more complicated than that. I should have guessed. At any rate, I remember perfectly well that he said, "It was Jonathan." Why would he have lied to me? It comes to me in a flash:

— It must be Kim then!

— Kim that what?

— Kim that killed Moisan.

There's a long silence. Bullseye! And if Kim hasn't taken off like we did, he must have been arrested by now. If we hurry, we'll make it back to the motel in time to catch the team bus back to Saint-Zéphyrin.

— No, it can't be Kim, says Jonathan, with all the conviction required to try to convince his dad that his best buddy isn't a murderer.

— Why? You know who killed him?

— No.

— Well what makes you say that, then?

Another long silence. Is Jonathan about to tell me he was there, that even though he didn't hit Don Moisan over the head he's still an accessory to murder? Not a bit of it.

He mumbles:

— Kim's a girl.

Now it's my turn to go quiet. Not for very long, then I ask:

— Are you sure?

— That she's a girl? Yeah.

Of course he's sure. She's going to have a hard time hiding that in a boys' locker room.

So Kim's a girl. It's true that he—she—looks more like a girl than a boy. For a second, just for a second, I swear, I regret not taking her up on the blow job.

What does it change that Kim's a girl? It's clear to Jonathan (and to me, after thinking about it for thirty seconds) that girls don't go round beating men to death with baseball bats. Look it up on Google or YouTube— "girl kills man with baseball bat"—and you won't get any hits. Not even worth checking.

So where does that leave me? Standing beside a long train track, with my son on the other side of the fence, not the murderer I had thought him to be. So the cops can't be after him. After me then? Even though I don't have a car anymore, I've kept a pile of unpaid tickets as a souvenir, but you don't send three cars for that kind of thing. Did the bastard coaching the Loons report me for inciting my players to violence? It doesn't make any sense, but it wouldn't be the first miscarriage of justice in the history of mankind or the biggest. The bastard must have known where the Zs were spending the night.

If that's what it is, the cops can't do much: interrogate me, then free me as long as I promise to appear in court. I'll have to ask Colombe to put up the bail, if there is one. She won't be pleased. Maybe I should ask my dad instead. I haven't spoken to him in ten years. In theory, it would be a good way to get back in touch: I can tell him I got arrested coaching a hockey team. In practice, I'm not sure he'd put his hand in his pocket to help me out.

Anyways, I'm not risking much and I'm the one the cops are after. And I'm starting to wonder if we'll ever find a hole in this damned fence if we keep heading this way.

— Right, back to the motel.
— You're going to turn yourself in?
— Yep.
— So what did you do? he insists.
— I can't tell you.
— I understand.

He looks convinced that I killed his ex-coach.

Why not let him believe it for a few more minutes? I bet I'm going up in his esteem. I'll be on my way back down again soon enough, if he finds out they're after me for traffic tickets. But in the meantime, it does both of us some good.

Jonathan hops back over the fence as easily as the first time and we keep walking, me in front.

We find our way back to the trail.

It's almost eight o'clock when we see the motel again. The cop cars have gone. I take out my key and open the door to Room 19, the one closest to us. Kim isn't there. Her equipment either. Room 18 is locked. Jonathan doesn't have the key. I ask him to knock and yell, just not too loud.

No answer.

— The bus has gone, says Jonathan.

I turn around. He's right: the bus has gone. It was parked near the office, most likely so as not to fill up the parking spots in front of the rooms.

So the aphasic has taken off with the rest of the team. Jonathan follows me to the office.

I go in. No one. I give the bell a tap. A woman comes out. From Mexico or somewhere else in Latin America, on the young and pretty side.

— Everyone gone?

— Yes. Everything's paid.

— The police arrest anyone?

She bursts out laughing. Then laughs some more. To get her to stop, I say:

— I don't see what's so funny.

— They come here to smoke a cigarette or two. They get a coffee from Tim Hortons on the other side of the highway. But they drink it here so no one sees them smoking.

I have woken my son up in the middle of the night, I have traipsed through a forest doing my best not to fall and break my neck in my leather-soled shoes, and all because of a bunch of nicotine-addicted cops?

— And one of them thinks I'm kinda cute, she adds.

She would have blushed if her skin hadn't already been so dark.

— All right, I say, like she needed my permission. Come on, Jonathan, we've got a call to make.

He follows me without asking who to. He's already guessed it's to his mom.

Colombe accepts the charges.

— What's going on?

— I'm with Jonathan. Everything's fine.

I had hoped that would be enough to calm her. Not by a long shot.

— Where are you? Beauchemin just called and said the two of you had disappeared and the bus had to leave without you.

— We're still in Morinville, outside the MoreInnTown Motel.

— What happened?

— Nothing. I'll explain later. But you'll have to come pick us up. I don't have enough money for the bus. I don't even know if there is one.

— I'm on my way.

She's not all that bad, Colombe. I don't regret marrying her, just not being married to her any longer. Always ready to help. I bet if I was here by myself she'd still jump into her Honda. I ask Jonathan:

— Any money on you?

— Twelve bucks.

— Let's go get some breakfast.

We take the overpass across highway and go into the Tim Hortons.

We eat our doughnuts in silence. I'm itching to ask Jonathan if he's in love with Kim. I bet he is. Even when I thought he was a boy, I thought he was a good-looking boy. But she's an even better-looking girl. Ten times better, because looking a bit effeminate is no longer a bad thing, far from it. But I don't see how to bring it up. It's none of my business. If I ask if Kim is his girl-friend, there's a one in two chance he'll says no, whether she is or not. For teens, nothing is more personal than their love lives. I could ask him if he was on heroin and I'd probably get a straighter answer.

And I'm sure he's itching to ask me if I'm ever going to get back together with Colombe.

I'd tell him no, even though I'd be only too happy to. She's as good-looking and sexy as ever. And if I had thought further than the end of my nose, I would never have cheated on her. Or I would at least have been more careful not to get caught. But how was I to know the electricity would go off at the sports bar in Taschereau while I was in bed with her intern?

Now that I'm an unemployed wreck, now's not the time to go into it all, not with her and not with our son either. What would I look like? The poor bum who wants to move back in with his ex until he pulls himself together and can start cheating on her again?

I order a second coffee. Jonathan doesn't want another hot chocolate. I'm glad he doesn't drink coffee. It proves he's still a kid. I don't know if you have any yourself, but teens are harder to love than children. And this morning I love my son like I always loved him when he was just a kid because he still is, a little. Let's hope it lasts.

A young family comes into the restaurant: a mom, dad, little girl, and a son the same age as Jonathan. The dad spots me and comes over:

— You dirty son of a bitch. I should call the cops on you.

— Be my guest.

I was kidding but he takes out his cell. Have rumours about the sex life of the Zs coach reached Morinville? Maybe he thinks I'm Don Moisan because he saw me at the arena last night. Better not stick around to find out.

— Come on, Jonathan. We're leaving.

It's almost eleven o'clock. Colombe won't be here for at least another hour. And Jonathan and I have run out of things to say to each other, after exhausting a few harmless subjects of conversation in the restaurant, from the chances it will rain (I predict sunny spells, while Jonathan predicts rain) to the chances of the Canadiens winning the Stanley Cup (non-existent, if you ask me; excellent, says Jonathan, but kids always tend to take their dreams for reality).

We go back to the front of the motel, beside the phone booth.

— Should be less than an hour now.

I mean Colombe, but I might as well have meant the rain because it starts raining. Jonathan has a waterproof jacket with him and insists I take shelter in the phone booth in my fleece jacket. If Colombe arrives and sees us standing there in the rain, me in the phone booth and Jonathan outside, what am I going to look like? I refuse.

The Latina girl gestures wildly for us to wait in the lobby. What will Colombe think if she sees me with a good-looking, olive-skinned young thing? I gesture that I'm waiting for a phone call. I say to Jonathan:

— You can wait in the motel, if you like.

— No, it's OK. It's not raining that hard.

I'd say it was raining hard enough. The Indian summer has just ended and the cold end-of-October rain has soaked through my jacket and shirt in next to no time. I'm having to make an effort to look stoical.

A green Honda eventually pulls up in front of us. I tell Jonathan:

— Go in the front.

— No, you.

For him it's natural for his mom and dad to sit beside each other in the car. He must even think that if we spend three hours like that, we'll end up back together.

I'd love nothing more, but there's not a chance. Colombe tells me, with the fieriness she reserves for whenever I've screwed up (which happens a lot), how worried she was this morning when she found out I'd disappeared with Jonathan. She'd even considered calling the police because she'd thought I might have kidnapped him and tried to cross the border. I protest:

— He would never have wanted to come.

— You think?

I couldn't be happier. Could it be that Jonathan not only wants to come live with me but get away from his mom too? Why not? I don't know how they manage it, together all those evenings, and the days too, every other weekend. You can say what you like but boys aren't

65

meant to live alone with their moms—not once puberty has hit both of them like a ton of bricks. The dad—even the worst dad in the world, i.e., me—is always going to be less strict. I never force Jonathan to make his bed before he goes back to his mom's, for one thing. That way he doesn't have to worry about rumpling the sheets twelve days later.

Colombe starts over again, for the fifth or sixth time, the same spiel but in different words and from a different angle (telling me what she said to her mom on the phone, for instance), telling me about what an awful morning she had, starting with the phone call from Beauchemin, who obviously told her I had coached the team for the night ("But you hate hockey. I thought he was pulling my leg.") and got a game misconduct.

— I knew it would end badly. Never do anything like that to me again.

I don't see how I could, even if I wanted to. Anyway, I don't see how it ended badly. Here we are in the Honda, alive if soaking wet, and we're not even being chased by the cops. I turn the heat up full blast. Colombe reaches over for a second to turn it down, but changes her mind and leaves it alone. She's not as angry as she looks.

And suddenly I feel like complaining too. What was she thinking? That I'd spent the night in a bar ogling the strippers? I say as matter-of-factly as I can, to take my revenge:

— We left the motel because I thought Jonathan had murdered his coach. And Jonathan thought that I'd done it.

Her jaw drops. For at least five minutes (OK, probably only two, but it feels like ten) she doesn't say a word.

I spend the time taking a good look at her out of the corner of my eye. She doesn't look a day older. Five years ago, I would have said she looked as old as I did. Now I'd say she was ten years younger. Like I was fifteen years older and she was five years younger. (Work it out for yourself, if you like. I might be wrong, but you get my point.)

I'd even say she was looking sexier than ever. Lots of women become more elegant with age, but precious few look sexier. If I didn't know her and met her in a bar, I'd definitely try to pick her up in the hopes of getting in her pants asap. If you could see her right leg, all thin, stretched toward the accelerator below a skirt that has slid back up to around mid-thigh level, you'd fall for her too.

After a long silence, Colombe replies with what seems like contained anger:

— And you can imagine Jonathan taking a baseball bat and hitting a man like Don Moisan over the head with it a dozen times, can you? And then snapping the bat in two and twisting the splintered shaft into his heart to finish him off?

I shake my head. No, Jonathan's not strong enough for that type of thing. Kim either, because I also thought it might have been her. But teenagers don't go around doing things like that. Fair enough, hitting someone over the head while he was trying to sexually assault you wouldn't be entirely out of the question. But then breaking the bat and plunging the shaft into a man's

67

heart? No. I can't see Jonathan or Kim doing that. And not just because of the strength it would take. It would take rage, most of all. Methodical rage. That takes an adult. An angry adult.

I bet you got there before I did: Colombe! And you're right: it could be Colombe. She's in shape. She did a half-marathon last year. She's aged well for a reason. And she's strong. I should know: she slapped me two or three times before kicking me out.

But most incriminating of all is what she just said. All I knew is that Don Moisan had been killed with a baseball bat. She said he had been finished off with a baseball bat to the heart. How would she know that? I have an idea to bring it all out into the open:

— Where was it?

She falls for it, even though I had been hoping she wouldn't walk straight into as obvious a trap:

— Beside the garage door behind his house. He got out of his car to open the door and someone who had been hiding in the bushes jumped him.

Ah no! It's as I feared: she does know. She knows how. She knows where. She knows everything. Because she did it. It can only be her. She found out—Jonathan or someone else told her—that Don Moisan was molesting her son. Personally, I would have called the police. Risking spending years in prison for bumping off a bastard like that? No thank you. Colombe can think straight too, but she has a fiery temper. Plus, a mother would get less than a man for a crime like that. And women's prisons are far better than men's. I saw one on TV once: not exactly a five-star hotel, but at least a

68

three-star one, better than the MoreInnTown at any rate. So she decided to take justice into her own hands and kill Moisan. No, it's not true: I think I could have murdered him too. When I found out what he had been doing to Jonathan, I would probably have felt like killing him if he hadn't already been dead. I'm glad he's dead: what more proof do you need? And I'm sure I'd be even gladder if I had killed him.

I feel like congratulating Colombe. Thanking her, while I'm at it. Saying something like, "Good job. If I'd known earlier, I would have done the same thing myself." But I know her. She'll just say, "What are you talking about?" She'll never admit to it. Partly because she doesn't trust me. She knows I'm no good at keeping a secret. And partly because Jonathan is in the back seat. A mother can't come right out in front of her son and say that she murdered someone, even if it was the man who was molesting him. Talk about shattering the essential but oh-so-fragile bond of trust between mother and teenage son. Especially since we'll never know what kind of relationship Jonathan and Don Moisan might have had together. Maybe there's a variant of Stockholm syndrome whereby a kid could more or less subconsciously hate their parent's guts if they killed their molester. Plus, if Colombe confides in him, she'll make him an accessory to murder. Maybe he could be accused after the fact. And me? Better to keep quiet about it all. That's what I'd do if I were Colombe.

We drive along in a heavy silence. To try to lighten the atmosphere and also because it sounds like congratulations (but not too much), I say:

— He got what he deserved.

The atmosphere isn't lightened by a single micropascal or any other atmospheric unit of measurement.

5

WE LEAVE THE HIGHWAY at the exit for Saint-Zéphyrin. There's a gas station where a litre of the precious liquid costs two or three cents less than at Old Caron's gas station downtown, at the only crossroads afflicted by traffic lights. Almost no one buys gas from Caron, not even when the light turns red. They only go there to inflate their bike tires for free (here it costs a dollar).

Colombe pulls up in front of the pumps without a word since it's obvious she's going to buy gas. She gets out of the car. I do too and I rush to beat her to the pump. I only have ten dollars or so left (Jonathan had enough money to pay for the Tim Hortons). Since I don't have enough money to pay for the gas she needed to come pick us up, the least I can do is make myself useful. But she takes the pump back off me.

— I can do it, she says.

Whatever she wants. I need a pee anyways. In ten minutes I'll be back home, where it'll be a lot cleaner. But I really need to go after those two coffees.

When I get back into the car, Colombe is in the booth, paying with her credit card. Jonathan doesn't speak. Me either. I force myself not to look at him. From the passenger seat I can't see him in the rear-view mirror anyways. To make conversation, I ask him:

— Hey, what's your team called?

He doesn't answer. Up to me to guess.

— It starts with a Z at any rate. The Zephyrs? The Zenith? The Zeroes? The Zappers?

I try to get him to laugh. But he's in no laughing mood. And I'm annoyed at myself for sounding like I was making fun of him.

There are days in a teen's life when nothing could be less funny than your dad's jokes. Colombe gets back in behind the wheel, finishes putting her credit card and receipt into her purse, and we're off again.

— Shall I leave you at your place?

— If you like.

It's almost three o'clock. She lives close by and I would have liked her to invite me round to her place for a drink and something to eat. I haven't eaten since the doughnuts in Morinville and my fridge is almost empty, as usual. Too bad.

The twelve kilometres that separate Saint-Zéphyrin and Saint-Camille speed by. Colombe slows down outside my place, puts her left-turn signal on, looks in the rear-view mirror to make sure no one's coming up behind her, and says, simply:

— Shit!

She turns left and around the abandoned gas pumps without stopping. I understood without even looking round: Jonathan isn't there. He took off on us at the gas station after the highway.

— I bet he's at Kim's, says Colombe. It's real close to my place.

I say, sounding like a bit of a know-it-all:

— Did you know that Kim's a girl?

— Of course I do. Doesn't everybody! Apart from the players on the other team, but it seems there's a few who know now. Jonathan says some of them are getting dirtier and dirtier with her. And not just because she's the best.

I've never played hockey, apart from two games I can't really remember, but I'm pretty sure that if I was playing against a girl who was better than I was, then I'd be tempted to send her flying over the boards by putting my stick between her legs too.

Like Colombe (and like me six months ago) Kim's family has a house in the suburbs, in a street that looks like any suburban street, in a neighbourhood everyone calls Chinatown, even though everyone who lives there was born and bred in Quebec. Or Vietnam. Or is a mix of the two. A good-looking woman, who's not at all Asian, answers the door no sooner have we rung the bell and hands us Jonathan's equipment bag, convinced that we've come to pick it up.

— Have you seen Jonathan? asks Colombe.

— He came to pick up Kim and told me to give you his bag. Kim brought it back with her.

I take it.

— Where did they go? Colombe asks again.

— I don't know.

Kim's mother cranes her neck to scan the lawn.

— They left on their bikes. Maybe ten, fifteen minutes ago now.

— Thanks.

We leave. I have an idea:

— Drop me off at my place. I'll get my bike and go have a look along the bike path.

— Good idea, agrees Colombe.

I'm proud of myself. You can't drive a car along the bike path, which is after all the first place to look when your son disappears with his girlfriend on his bike.

We go up into my apartment to check that Jonathan isn't there, I exchange my coat for my old leather jacket and pedal the ten kilometres of the bike path between Saint-Camille and Saint-Zéphyrin as fast as I can. After Saint-Zéphyrin, it goes on to Taschereau, but there's no reason why Kim and Jonathan would be there. I leave from the other end, where the path ends at the foot of the wooded hills just behind Saint-Camille, a stone's throw from the giant cow. I don't see Jonathan's white mountain bike. (I got him a white one so that I could write "All white, Jonathan?" on the card he got for his fourteenth birthday, although he barely cracked a smile.)

In fact, I don't see a single bike apart from mine. It stopped raining an hour or two ago, but at the end of October the bike path is still deserted. Where have Jonathan and Kim gotten to? I have no idea, and I don't really care either. I'm much more worried about Colombe.

Because the more I think about it, the surer I am that she killed that bastard Don Moisan. And I really don't want her to get herself arrested. It would all be so much easier if I had done it. I'm unemployed and a mediocre dad, while Colombe earns a good living and is doing a better job bringing up Jonathan by herself than I ever could. If Colombe had to go to prison for a year or two, I'd have to find myself a job, learn to cook, and take care of Jonathan to boot. I suppose I'd manage. But it wouldn't be easy for either of us.

It really would be better if I got sentenced for it. I wouldn't get that long—a year or two—for killing the coach who had been abusing my son, Kim, and maybe others on the team.

And the best-case scenario would be if they gave me a suspended sentence to serve in the community. I'd be willing to do anything at all, as long as it didn't have anything to do with hockey. Pick up empty beer cans along the road or clear the park with the giant cow in it, which looks nothing like a park because it is so over-grown. I could even repaint the cow, which is getting to be really rusty, as long as they supply the paint and brushes.

And if I do manage to get accused of murder, the best is still to come: Colombe would be eternally grateful for having been spared a trial and a prison sentence. (The sentence would no doubt have been lighter for her, but there's another reason to thank me.) And while I'm dreaming, maybe we'd get back together when I got out. I'd swear to be faithful and true and I think I'd manage—things must get easier after you turn forty.

I must admit a life like that doesn't sound too much like a barrel of laughs. But the life I'm leading at the minute isn't hilarious either. And I'd feel like a hero. No, I'd be a hero.

Straight out. The man who gave it all up for his wife and child.

I leave the bike path and pedal through the centre of Saint-Zéphyrin until I reach the police station. I let my bike fall down onto the pavement in the parking lot. No point locking it to a telephone pole. No one's mad enough to steal a bike from right under the noses of the police. And I don't care if anyone takes off with it anyway. You work out in prison; you don't go cycling.

I push the door open and walk up to the counter. I cough to get the attention of the young lady in uniform sitting in front of a computer. She raises her eyes.

— I've come about the murder of Don Moisan.

— Take a seat over there.

She points to a row of chairs, where someone is sitting already.

— It's urgent, I say, because it doesn't seem to me that a murderer who wants to turn himself in but neglects to declare his intentions should have to cool his heels in a police station any more than someone who is dying should have to wait in a hospital emergency room.

— Everyone thinks everything is always urgent all the time, says the woman with the contempt of someone who thinks they're dealing with someone who has just had their car stolen.

I decide not to say any more. I want to confess—a false confession is still a confession, right?—but to

76

someone more receptive, not to a young woman who's looking down her nose at me like I'd just offered her a drink in a bar.

I sit down beside a guy my age. He seems nervous and keeps playing around with a cigarette that he's not smoking. I don't see any signs, but I seriously doubt you're allowed to smoke in a police station in the second decade of the twenty-first century. I would have tried to strike up a conversation with him, but a door opens, a man comes out—around thirty-five or forty as well—and the man who was waiting with me walks in to replace him.

I regret not bringing a book or my MP3 player. At any rate, I have to think about what I'm going to say. And just as I've more or less made up my mind, the door opens again, my predecessor walks out, and a plain clothes cop motions for me to come in.

I sit down across from a big guy with glasses. Either younger than me or my age and in better shape.

— Detective Lieutenant Provençal, he says, even though there's a plate with his name on it on his desk: Det. Lt. S. Provençal.

I introduce myself:

— Antoine Vachon.

— I know.

I recognize him. He's already stopped me for speeding. He was in uniform then. I suppose he must have got a promotion to be plain clothes now. I feel reassured: patrol officers have to sit exams before they can become investigators. So my cop has every chance of being less incompetent than average.

— What can I do for you? he asks, with a hint of irritation that is perfectly understandable if he hasn't forgotten I called him every name under the sun when he arrested me.

But he looks exhausted, as though he's been working all night. Maybe he's the cop Beauchemin told me about. If he is tired, putting my plan into action will be easier. I attack:

— I killed Don Moisan.

— Oh right...

He sounds blasé, like he arrested dozens of murderers every week.

— My son is on his hockey team (I would have preferred to say "My son plays for the..." but I still don't know the team's name) and he told me his coach was molesting some of the players. Not him, but some of the other players.

You'll have noticed that I want to avoid revealing that Jonathan was one of them. He'd never forgive me for heaping shame upon him like that. Victims are always like that. Especially fourteen-year-old boys. I go on:

— I hate pedophiles. I was molested as a boy.

It's not true, but it gives me some credibility. Although, come to think of it, molesters are often former victims and now he might think I'm one myself. But it's too late to make up for my blunder, if a blunder it was.

— And how did you murder him?

— I couldn't sleep after everything my son had said. He told me where his coach lived...

— What was the address again?

— I can't remember. He just showed me his house once when we passed by it. I took my baseball bat and went to wait for him, hidden behind the garage. When he arrived, I waited until he got out of his car. And I jumped him and hit him over the head with my bat. Then I took the end of the broken bat and plunged it into his heart to be real sure he was dead.

— Can you give me any more details? Like what he was wearing?

That's the problem with my statement. I came up with it as best I could on my bike and waiting outside Lieutenant Provençal's door. There are loads of details missing. All I know is what Colombe told me. Fortunately, I came prepared:

— I'm not saying another word, not without a lawyer. But I can sign a statement, if you like.

— No thank you. It's hardly worth it.

We both go quiet. He hasn't written down a word of what I said. He's saving it for the interrogation. He'll have a stenographer and a video camera, everything he needs to worm it out of me and make sure it will stand up in front of a judge, even if I decide to deny it all in court. All criminals do that, and I'll do the same to add to my credibility, even if—especially if—my lawyer tells me not to.

For the time being I need to avoid going into detail. I've never seen Don Moisan. I don't know if he's tall, fat, old, young, if he has a moustache or a beard. I need to get the lieutenant to talk so I can repeat everything he tells me back to him without him noticing. It's no easy task, but not impossible if I concentrate. When you want to be a hero, you have to pay the price and that takes some effort.

He holds my gaze for a while, like he was trying to read my thoughts, then looks away and sighs as though overcome by weariness, like he was getting ready to ask me for a pay raise because he's so exhausted:

— But what's the matter with you all today?

I don't know what he means by "you all." He goes on to explain:

— Do you know that you're the fifth person today? I should have you arrested for wasting police time.

Me, wasting police time? There's a little truth in that, I suppose, since I'm trying to divert suspicion away from my wife and onto me.

But how can he be so sure? He doesn't waste any time telling me:

— I'm not going to waste my time worming it out of you. I'm going to leave the worms well alone and give it to you straight. Last Thursday a couple of players on your son's team had a meeting and decided to speak to their parents. Two of them were being sexually abused. One of them was a girl pretending to be a boy because this Bantam B league doesn't let girls play on boys' teams, even though no girls teams play higher than pee-wee. The boys suspected the girl of being pregnant, which was the straw that broke the camel's back. She was being sick in the locker-room toilets. They decided to tell their parents, but making them promise not to reveal the girl's identity. She was their top scorer, all they wanted was to be rid of their coach, preferably to see him behind bars. And Don Moisan was killed that same night, beaten to death with a baseball bat. It was the night of Thursday to Friday. This morning, the local newspaper printed an article containing a few details. And ever since then a few crackpots like you have been acting the hero, swearing that you killed him. There was even a woman that tried to convince me she did it, as if a woman could ever kill a man like that. Did you ever see Don Moisan?

He pauses in the hope that I'll shake my head. I'm not stupid enough to fall for that one: I don't even blink.

— A retired military police sergeant. Six foot three, two hundred eighty pounds. He would have ripped the baseball bat out of your hands and stuck it where the sun don't shine.

Suddenly I feel better. Colombe didn't do it. I should have known. She doesn't look like a murderer. Me either, by the looks of things.

I risk a question, just to put my mind completely at rest:

— What are you going to do?

He gives me a tired smile before answering:

— For the past two years, the Devil's Own biker gang has been keeping us busy twenty-eight hours a day, nine days a week. They have extended their territory up this far, because they're starting to have too many problems in Montreal. They control the production and distribution of every drug imaginable. Now they're involved in prostitution, loan sharking, even Ponzi schemes and false billing. Not to mention the restaurant protection racket. There would need to be a hundred of us to be able to do anything. There are only fourteen of us. Do you think we're going to waste much time looking for whoever murdered some bastard of a pedophile who got a little girl pregnant? There are twenty players on the team. Each player has one or two parents who would have been perfectly justified… You promise you won't say a word about any of this to the press?

This time I shake my head enthusiastically. To remove all possible doubt, I mime zipping my mouth shut.

— I'm only telling you all this because I know your ex-wife. Don't repeat it to anyone. Thirty moms and dads would have been perfectly justified in killing the scumbag. With a little luck, in a few months we'll find a Devil's Own we can't pin anything else on and we'll try to get him to take the fall. It'll be even better if he happens to be one of the players' dads, but it doesn't really matter. He might even plead guilty so that he can look the part in front of all his buddies. Those guys think a pedophile killer is a real hero, even though they wouldn't think twice about forcing a fourteen-year-old girl into prostitution themselves. But that's another story. And if we don't find the murderer, real or imagined, then we'll just close the case. It won't be the first time. Or the last.

He closes his eyes. To show me the conversation is now over or because he's really fallen asleep?

I leave without making a sound.

6

I LEAVE THE POLICE STATION in good spirits. They didn't arrest me let alone convict me. Colombe either. And Jonathan's name won't be appearing in the papers.

All's well that ends well. I get back on my bike. But I haven't even kicked the pedal when Colombe's Honda roars into the parking lot and pulls up in front of me. I drop my bike again and walk over. She lowers the window on her side. I'm getting ready to joyfully announce that all is well in the best of all possible worlds. But she doesn't give me the chance to open my mouth.

— Well, did they find them?

I've forgotten the one black cloud in my blue sky: Jonathan has disappeared with Kim. Kim, who's pregnant by her coach as I've just learned and which I'll be telling Colombe the first chance I get. I'd rather his mother broke the news to Jonathan. And I forgot to tell the police about the disappearance of our two teenagers. Not that I'm going to admit that to Colombe. They wouldn't do anything anyway. I've seen enough American movies to know that they won't look for anyone—apart from babies—until they've been missing for twenty-four hours.

Here it must take at least a week. Especially when there's fourteen of them instead of a hundred.

— No, they're making inquiries but they're swamped, what with the Devil's Own and now Don Moisan into the bargain. They're not interested in kids who have been missing for an hour.

— Come on, we'll try to find them ourselves. They're not at my place and I've been to check at their friends'. They're not there either.

I leave my bike where it is. It's almost winter anyways and if I move back in with Colombe I wouldn't be needing it again. I hop back in beside her, and when we're on the road again to Saint-Camille, she says:

— Where do you think young ones would go to commit suicide around here?

— What? Suicide?

She needs to spell it out to me.

— Jonathan and Kim are in love.

The thought had never crossed my mind. I knew they were friends, but in love? (Although if Colombe says it, it must be true.)

— So?

— Ever read Romeo and Juliet?

I say yes, even though it's been too long for me to remember, probably because I've never read it.

— It wouldn't surprise me if they've made a suicide pact. I'm sure they don't know what's going on any more with all this talk of murder and the rest of it.

Colombe is right. And she doesn't know that Don Moisan got Kim pregnant. Should I tell her? I don't think I should. She goes on:

84

— If I'd known…

— If you'd known what?

She hesitates. She really doesn't want to go on.

I insist:

— Known what?

— Five or six months ago, it must have been March or April, you'd just moved and Jonathan asked me if Kim could stay over. I said no. Not until he was sixteen.

Did I mention that Colombe and I both lost our virginity at eighteen? Not together, but both at the same age. I don't remember who with, but it was on the back seat of her dad's Buick. If you ask me, Colombe would have preferred Jonathan to wait another four years, not two. But she settled on a fair compromise: not until he was sixteen. Two more years. She doesn't seem so sure anymore:

— If I'd said yes, then maybe they'd be happy.

I refrain from protesting that while screwing may be fun, it doesn't necessarily make you happy, especially when you're in your teens.

— Where would you go? she asks.

— Where would I go…?

— If you wanted to commit suicide with your girl-friend?

I don't know. I've never wanted to kill myself. Although I could have. Maybe even should have when Colombe kicked me out the very same week I got the news that Saturns and Pontiacs were both going to disappear.

If I wanted to commit Harry Carry, I think I'd try to drown myself. By jumping from the bridge right in the middle of Saint-Zéphyrin, around four o'clock in the morning when nobody could help me without asking first. I can't swim and it seems a fairly painless way to go. Swallowing water. And it must all be over with in two or three minutes, unless you're unlucky enough to do it in front of a good Samaritan who drags you back to shore and gives you mouth to mouth.

But Jonathan swims like a fish. I signed him up for swim club in the hopes that it would keep him away from hockey. It didn't work for very long, but he did learn to swim and it's like riding a bike: you never forget. And I bet your survival instinct takes over if you jump into the water to kill yourself when you know how to swim.

Jonathan doesn't have a car, so there's no carbon monoxide at his disposal. Or pillars to crash into. No poison that I know of. His mother and I don't take any drugs. And it seems unlikely that two teens would overdose on Colombe's contraceptive pills, if she's still taking them at thirty-nine. We don't have a gas cooker. There's no nearby cliff to jump off. Throw themselves under a train? The railway track is now a bike path between Taschereau and the cow. Hey, the cow, and I say:

— The cow.

— The cow?

— Yes, the cow.

Colombe gets it and soon we're racing along the road to Saint-Camille. You might be wondering what cow we're talking about. I'll explain everything, even if I've already mentioned it, and it will give me a chance to tell you all about my village's history, which ordinarily you wouldn't want to know anything about.

Camille Simoneau was the first farmer to set up home in Saint-Camille-de-Holstein, round about 1905. It wasn't called that back then. It wasn't called anything at all. When the parish was formed around 1916, with the influx of young city folk looking to flee conscription into the army, the local priest wanted to pay tribute to his most illustrious parishioner, since Camille Simoneau had been the first to show that you could survive and prosper in a place where hay was the only thing not in short supply. He named the parish and the village Saint-Camille. A few years later, they found out there was another Saint-Camille in the Eastern Townships. It had been founded in 1848 and had priority. To set itself apart, my village was renamed Saint-Camille-de-Châteaubriand, after the county it was in.

A few uneventful decades passed, until the electoral map was redrawn, sending Saint-Camille-de-Châteaubriand into the next riding. Camille Junior, the eldest son of the Camille we know and mayor of the village, held a referendum, which he won hands down, and from then on—and forever after, by the looks of things—the village was known as Saint-Camille-de-Holstein, as a tribute to all the prizes won by local Holstein cows in agricultural shows. Holsteins still win plenty of prizes for their well-to-do breeders to this day, and back then Camille Junior was chief among them.

When the highway was built—without an exit for Saint-Camille, which had had the misfortune of voting en masse for the PartI Québécois (with Camille Junior the unfortunate PQ candidate at the previous election)—Camille Junior, him again, decided that the village needed something that could be seen from the highway to encourage tourists to come buy gas, beer, unpasteurized cream, and cheese curds there.

And so the municipality had a huge sheet-metal reproduction of a Holstein cow made, which was put up on the hill between the village and the highway.

The fifteen-metre-high black and white structure was set down on four posts that were also fifteen metres in height, so that the friendly beast appeared to be floating above the forest.

Personally I can't think of anything in poorer taste than to jump off something so ridiculous, but Colombe seems convinced that kids of today would find the whole thing incredibly romantic.

She's speeding along, but it doesn't stop me thinking things over. Because a coincidence has suddenly popped into my head. And I'm not so sure it's a coincidence.

I've remembered there was a Provençal-Latendresse on Jonathan's team. Now do you remember the name of the cop who put my mind at ease by telling me I'd never be a suspect in the investigation because the police couldn't care less about finding Don Moisan's murderer?

Congratulations: you have an excellent memory. His name was Provençal. And I wouldn't be at all surprised if he was the murderer. Provençal must be buddy buddy with his line-mates. (I can remember that perfectly as well— Line 1: K. Nguyen, Vachon, Latendresse-Provençal.)

Is he the cop's son?

Not necessarily: there must be a dozen Provençals in Saint-Zéphyrin, starting with the mayor, who's old enough to be my cop's dad. How can I find out?

Nothing could be easier. On my left is an excellent source that will tell me everything I need to know. Colombe is the head of the biggest accounting firm in Saint-Zéphyrin. She prepares the tax returns for three out of every four adults who live there. And each tax return contains a ton of information. Including how many children the taxpayer has. And maybe even their first names on a prescription or two. So do you think I should give her the third degree?

Well, I'm going to, whether you want me to or not.

— By the way, Provençal, the cop, do you know him well?

I don't get an answer right away. But Colombe takes her foot off the accelerator. No doubt trying to remember which of the cops living in and around Saint-Zéphyrin might be called Provençal. But I'm wrong, because after thinking for a minute, she admits:

— I was going to tell you soon anyway. Might as well tell you now. Stéphane and I are moving in together in a few weeks. You know the old stone house by the river, not far from the bridge? We're going to buy it. Stéphane has a son, the same age as Jonathan. You know him: they're on the same line. I'm sure they'll be the best of friends. It won't change anything for you, of course. You'll still have Jonathan every other weekend.

She steps on the gas again and goes back up to a hundred and ten in an eighty zone, like every cop's girlfriend who knows she'll never get a ticket.

That bastard Provençal! I don't give a damn if he's the murderer now or not. It's worse than that: he's stolen my wife. OK, so we're separated and divorce proceedings are well underway. But until the divorce comes through, in the eyes of the law she's still my wife, not his. And to top it all, they're going to live in the nicest house for miles around. While I stay in my miserable bachelor above a contaminated garage.

The worst thing about it all is that one day Jonathan will give in to temptation and call him "Dad" just to please him. I bet Colombe and loverboy will have a pool put in too—with two teens in a house with the income of a chartered accountant and a police lieutenant, you more or less have to have one.

I'll never see Jonathan again in the summer. A pool attracts friends. Girls especially. To console me, Colombe will invite me over for a swim too. But I won't be able to bear the sight of Colombe lounging around in a bikini by the pool while her new husband barbecues the steaks. (She didn't say they were going to get married, but it's inevitable if you ask me—just last week she told me to get a move on signing the divorce papers I could find if I looked a bit harder.) And he'll burn mine to a crisp, even if I ask for it rare.

I try to forget the horrors running through my head while Colombe, me beside her in the passenger seat, drives full throttle toward the cow, speeding through Saint-Camille without ever slowing down, like any driver passing through for the first time, whether they're going out with a cop or not.

Here we are then at the start of the path up to the cow. There's a little overgrown park, completely deserted in this season ill-suited to picnics.

I get out of the car, reassured since I don't see the bikes belonging to the two lovebirds, if lovebirds they are. I'm even just about to get back in the car, but Colombe presses the button on her key ring to lock the doors.

— Let's go have a look, she orders.

If that's what she wants. We take a few steps and I'm unlucky enough to look behind me and see two bikes hiding in the bushes, out of sight of any passing thieves, even though it's obvious thieves never pass by here. My first reflex is to keep my mouth shut, but then I think Colombe will just see them herself on the way back and be annoyed I didn't say anything.

— Colombe...

She's a few steps ahead of me. She turns round and sees the bikes.

— That's Jonathan's, I say, without even pointing at the white one.

She recognizes it too, and hurries back toward the hill. I can hardly keep up with her.

Good news: no teens lying flattened underneath the cow. Colombe stops at the bottom of the ladder and looks up. The ladder has I don't know how many steps. It's around twenty or twenty-five metres up to the cow's stomach.

— They must be up there.

I cup my hands round my mouth, but Colombe whispers before I can call out to Jonathan:

— No. Go have a look instead.

Jonathan's going to jump to his death if I call him? Not a chance in a hundred, if you ask me. But even if it was a chance in a thousand, it wouldn't be worth taking.

Colombe is afraid of heights. I am too, but less than her. It's up to me to go up. All the more so since it fits perfectly with the new role of hero I'd like to take on. Especially in front of Colombe, now that I have to compete with everybody's favourite hero: a cop fighting the Devil's Own with absolutely no chance of coming out on top—which only makes him look even more heroic.

A rusty red notice screwed to the ladder warns that trespassers will be fined. But it's not stopped anybody yet and nobody's ever had to pay a fine.

I take a deep breath and put my hands on a rung around chest height. It's cold and made out of iron. I need gloves but I don't have any. At least it's not cold enough for the rain on the rungs to have frozen. I climb up, forcing myself not to look up or down. But after a good dozen steps, I risk a glance at Colombe. She puts her finger over her mouth to remind me not to make any noise. I'm halfway up, then soon at the top. I stop for a minute. What should I do? What should I say? "Hi there, kids. You're not going to jump, are you?" Why not: "Hey, is your team the Zippos or the Zena Warrior Princesses, then?"

I do what I'm told and stay quiet. There is a rectangular opening into the cow. It's covered by a removable metal plate. When I was Jonathan's age, I would come up here with my buddies. Never any girls, they always said they were too scared—probably of us jumping on them as much as falling. On both flanks there are also huge panels you can open to admire the countryside through. One day a tourist dropped his dog and sued the municipality; the mayor had the "No Trespassing" sign added to the ladder.

I go up another step. I put my ear to the plate. Not a sound. They're not there. While I'm there, I take a good look around me. They're not down below either, anywhere I can see them anyway.

Hey, there's a noise inside the cow. Sounds like breathing. Then a conversation I can barely make out:

— You don't regret it?

— No. What else could we have done?

— I know. Do you still love me?

— Of course I do. And you?

— I love you so much.

I can hear the whispers through the cow's metal stomach. I'm not sure who's who. I think I heard Jonathan first, or it might have been Kim. Hard to say. But I know it's them.

At any rate, the appallingly trite exchange they probably have a hundred times a day is followed by the unmistakable sound of creaking metal. They're screwing. Can my Jonathan, my baby of just over fourteen, really be getting it on when I'd barely discovered masturbation at his age? It sure sounds like it. The kids of today, eh?

Fourteen-year-olds are less wet behind the ears today than we were at seventeen. And what else can they do but screw, as Kim (or Jonathan) just pointed out? Sex is everywhere they look: in ads, movies, video games...

All doubt is soon removed as the creaking is lost to the sounds of heavy breathing. I practically have a hard-on, like I'm listening to a porno flick without seeing what's going on, which is even more arousing, as you'll know if you've ever done it. I'm not about to push back the metal plate and go "Hello! Only me!"

Instead I decide to go back down without making a sound. They're fourteen, they can do what they want. The only thing they're not allowed to do, I think, is sleep with someone younger: I'm pretty sure the law says a five-year age gap if one of them's a minor. They're the same age. Two steps further down I remember that Kim is pregnant by her coach. Another three steps and I realize it wasn't her coach at all, like everyone else on the team thought. It's Jonathan's baby! She must have told Don Moisan "I only do blow jobs" too, like she did with me. That's not how a girl gets pregnant. And now I know why she said yes in the motel when I asked her if it was Jonathan. She wasn't saying he had killed Don Moisan, she meant he was the father of her baby. Maybe she had been sick in the bathroom and thought I had heard her. Or I might have noticed her bump was starting to show under her massive pyjamas.

In the end it's just as well it's Jonathan's and not Don Moisan's baby. I keep going down, despite Colombe motioning at me to go back up and open the metal plate. No, I'll leave them to it.

With every rung I mull over my new discoveries. Kim will need an abortion. Even if her parents don't want her to, I think she's allowed to have an elective abortion. But what if she doesn't want to?

She'd be mad not to. She's only fourteen: having a baby would ruin her whole life. Although not necessarily. Especially if I help them. I only have one bedroom but I could sleep on the couch. I'll find a crib in a garage sale somewhere. If she wants to keep her baby—my grandson, I've just realized—she'll probably have to miss a year of school. But as soon as the baby's a couple of months old, I'll be able to look after it and she can go on with her studies. Especially since her dad's Vietnamese, and Asians never let their kids leave school without a diploma—preferably a PhD.

Better yet I could talk Colombe into leaving Stéphane and letting us all move in with her. Especially if she buys the old house by the river. She's bound to be able to afford it on her own. It's huge. If she insists, we could sleep in separate rooms until I convince her I can stop snoring. Apparently you can now, if you get a load of special tubes to stick up your nose at night.

The main thing is for the kids to feel their parents are behind them. That's why kids going through what they're going through end up killing themselves: they feel like the whole world has let them down. Convincing Colombe's probably not going to be easy. I know her, she'll push hard for an abortion. And she's right as well. Kim's parents too. But if Kim and Jonathan want to keep their baby, that's up to them. Even if they won't be able to get by on their own. They have my support—I'd go as far as to say they have my complete support— whatever they decide. Especially since there aren't enough births in Quebec as it is. One more abortion is one too many.

I only have a few minutes to talk Colombe into supporting them too. They're not going to be at it for hours, all the same. As soon as they climb down from their sheet-metal love nest, we'll have to be ready to tell them they can count on us no matter what.

Ah, I've got one foot on terra firma. And a second. I turn to Colombe, who looks mad as hell. She's going to be even madder in a minute or two.

— Are they there?

— Yes.

— What are they doing?

I try to ease the tension in the air a little before breaking the bad news:

— They're doing what we should be doing too.

I want to press myself against her, but I should take things slowly. If I play my cards right and don't rush things I'll be in bed with Colombe tonight. Or in a few days. I put my hands on her shoulders. I'm off to a good start: she doesn't push me away, just frowns. I murmur:

— They're making love.

She doesn't get mad. She looks relieved, if anything. While I'm at it, I add:

— She's pregnant.

It's a miracle: she's not angry. OK, tears well up in her eyes, but she smiles. Like she's delighted to be a grandmother at thirty-nine. She says:

— If she wants to keep it, I'll help her.

— Me too.

She doesn't point out that my unemployed "me too" doesn't mean much. I'll have to explain that I mean I'll help take care of the baby. I'm relieved. It will be easier to support Kim, Jonathan, and their baby if Colombe's helping too and I'm not on my own. We'll move in with her, in her house in Chinatown or in the new house by the river, and I'll look after the house while Kim's at school. I'll even cook and clean. Once the baby is born and weaned, Kim will go back to school and I'll keep an eye on him. That's something. I might be broke, but I can at least make myself useful. And it'll teach that bastard Provençal to have a full-time job with tons of overtime.

I open my arms and Colombe rests her head on my shoulder. And hope springs eternal. I feel like swearing my eternal loyalty. But now's not the time. She'd never believe me and it would spoil the moment I've been dreaming about for the past six months.

We stand there, leaning against each other. I pat her back. We hear a creaking sound and look back up at the huge cow. We can't see anything. It's not the metal plate or the panel on our side. It must be the one on the other side. Our lovebirds have finished and are now admiring the scenery below. From the other side you can't see the village, but the Appalachians are on the horizon, on the other side of the highway, and everything looks much nicer with the autumn leaves, even if three-quarters of them have disappeared by now.

I look at Colombe. I don't really know what to say. She's emotional and I am too. That doesn't happen to me as often. I'm not really used to it. I open my mouth to say "I still love you, you know." But I don't have time to say it, because she yells:

— Noooo!

Before I can turn right round, I hear a dull thud. A noise I've never heard before, but right away I recognize the sound of two bodies crashing against the ground. Colombe pushes me away and starts running. Before I've turned round, I try to hope it's not Jonathan and Kim. I didn't see them, I only heard their voices. Maybe I was wrong. If it was young Latendresse-Provençal and his girlfriend, that would be perfect. But I don't believe it for a second.

I still need to go look. My feet are heavy. I drag them over to where the two naked bodies are lying in the grass. They're still holding hands. Jonathan is lying flat on his face. Kim too, but her head has dislocated and is looking up at the sky, her eyes open. They jumped head first. I suppose that's the way to go when you want to make sure.

I take Colombe's hand. She shakes it loose. All she says is what women often say whenever disaster strikes:

— I knew it.

How could she have known?

I didn't know anything about it. I still don't know anything. I don't even know why the name of the team I coached last night starts with a Z. Above all else, I'm wondering why Kim and Jonathan decided to die together at fourteen.

Did they kill Don Moisan? He was big and tall, but maybe Kim distracted him while Jonathan hit him over the head from behind. Or maybe it wasn't premeditated at all. Don Moisan wanted to bring them both home with him. He tried to kiss Kim or feel her up or rape her and Jonathan found a baseball bat lying around.

No, that doesn't make any sense. Perhaps you thought of it too: when Jonathan ran away from the motel with me, he asked me why the cops were after me. If he had killed Moisan, he would have been sure they were after him, not me. If you ask me, that proves he was innocent.

But what does it matter if he did it, or Kim did it, or Colombe did it, or I did it? Or Detective Lieutenant Provençal? Another hockey mom or dad? A group of outraged parents? Or just a drunk on his way past who felt like hearing the sound a skull makes when you hit it hard enough?

Knowing isn't going to bring my Jonathan back.

And yet you'd think having conceived a kid would have given them a bit of a boost, especially Jonathan, who didn't have to carry it around with him all the time. But maybe not, not when you're fourteen and your mom doesn't want you to sleep with your girlfriend for another two years. And when your dad is out of work and irresponsible and you're sure he wouldn't be able to help anyway.

Could I have stopped them? If I had opened the panel and said "Right, that's enough, you two, come on down," would they have followed or said "Give us two minutes to get dressed," and jumped when I was waiting for them at the bottom of the ladder?

I don't know if I'm a little bit responsible, or a lot responsible, or not at all.

I don't know if it's going to change my life either. I don't know if it's going to smooth things out with Colombe, or make them worse. She needs me now more than ever. She'll start by pushing me away. How long can she keep it up? Not for too long if I squeal on that bastard Provençal, who the more I think about it probably did murder Don Moisan. As everybody knows, trash murders trash.

But even if it really was him, he's still a cop and cops are good at covering each other's backs. All it takes is for another cop to swear before a judge that the accused was beside him in a police car on the night of the crime. I'd rather keep my suspicions to myself. Colombe would never believe me, anyways: a woman in love could never imagine her boyfriend was a murderer.

But what am I going to do with no Colombe and no Jonathan?

I don't know if I'm going to become an alcoholic or a schizophrenic, a hooligan or a homeless bum in some Montreal park. Unless I climb up into the cow and spend the winter there. I could kick the ladder away so I'd be stuck up there.

But I don't know if I could do it.

To be honest, I know diddly-squat right now.

Apart from one thing I've always known. And now I know it more than ever...

I HATE hockey!

FICTION AND CREATIVE NONFICTION

Roads to Richmond: Portraits of Quebec's Eastern Townships by Nick Fonda

Break Away: Jessie on my mind by Sylvain Hotte

You could lose an eye, My first 80 years in Montreal by David Reich

Principals & Other Schoolyard Bullies, Short Stories by Nick Fonda

HISTORY AND POLITICAL ISSUES

Barack Obama and the Jim Crow Media,
The return of the nigger breakers by Ishmael Reed

A People's History of Quebec by Jacques Lacoursière & Robin Philpot

America's Gift, What the world owes to the Americas
and their first inhabitants by Käthe Roth and Denis Vaugeois

The Question of Separatism, Quebec and the Struggle
over Sovereignty by Jane Jacobs

An Independent Quebec, The past, the present and the future by Jacques Parizeau

Joseph-Elzéar Bernier, Champion of Canadian
Arctic Sovereignty by Marjolaine Saint-Pierre

Trudeau's Darkest Hour, War Measures in time of peace, October 1970
edited by Guy Bouthillier & Édouard Cloutier

The Riot that Never Was
The military shooting of three Montrealers in 1832
and the official cover-up by James Jackson

Discrimination in the NHL, Quebec Hockey Players Sidelined by Bob Sirois

Inuit and Whalers on Baffin Island through German Eyes,
Wilhelm Weike's Arctic Journal and Letters (1883-1884)
by Ludger Müller-Wille & Bernd Gieseking, Translated by William Barr

Printed in Canada
on Enviro 100% recycled
at Lebonfon Printing.